THE JOURNEYMAN

BookLocker.com, Inc.
2010

THE JOURNEYMAN

Mickey Thompson

Acknowledgements

Thomas Gilgut Jr.
Editor and Friend

Rose Droge
Manuscript Preparation

Al Califano
Author's Photo

Rev. Msgr. John Brinn
Poughkeepsie Connection

THE ELECTRICIAN

Chris Brown pulled into the office parking lot fully prepared for the new week. There were three cases pending and he knew he had done his homework; this would be a good week. As always he had been listening to what his daughter called 'Dad's alternative radio station' and drinking coffee from the travel mug his wife had purchased for him. Chris always sat in the parking lot for ten or fifteen minutes before heading into the office. He liked to get to work early and collect his thoughts as opposed to rushing in late and breathless.

The weekend had been a smashing success. As the coach of the Newburgh Hawks Little League team, he had brought them through with a record of 18-0-0. So here he sat, a great weekend and a promising week ahead. Chris finished his last sip of coffee, opened his car door, smiled to himself and was ready to take on the world.

The law offices of Brown and Brown were small in size yet business had never been better. Chris loved the first half hour of his morning which left him alone and the thinking came easy. Should the phone ring, Chris had no problem with playing secretary. He could remember the first year and a half when there was no money for a secretary. He also remembered who did the floors and windows back then, too.

After about forty-five minutes the phone rang. Chris answered with the usual greeting, "Good morning, Brown and Brown." After saying good morning he quickly checked his watch and thought: it's still morning, I knew that.

The voice of a woman replied, "Good morning, may I speak to Jane or Chris Brown?"
"This is Chris Brown. How may I help you?"

"I don't know if you remember me but we met about six months ago. Your wife introduced us at her graduation. My husband was in her class, Fozi Al Fozie. My name is Marie Al Fozie."

Chris flashed to the introduction remembering how her husband's name repeated itself and that he was dressed in Middle Eastern garb. Marie was dressed like the all-American girl and that seemed strange.

"How are you, Marie? How is Fozi?" said Chris.

There was a slight pause and then Marie answered, "That's what I would like to talk to you about."

"Is everything alright, Marie?" Chris offered.

"Could I make an appointment, Mr. Brown?" she went on to say.

"Marie, please call me Chris, and when is good for you?"

"Please Mr. Brown, Chris, the sooner the better." Marie began to sound desperate.

"One second, Marie." After checking his appointment book he asked if Tuesday at nine would be good.

Answering promptly she spit out, "That will be great and I can't thank you enough!"

"So I will see you tomorrow morning then," Chris ended.

After Chris hung up he thought he had detected sadness in Marie Al Fozie's voice. He caught himself thinking, I hope this is not a divorce issue. Brown and Brown was about investment matters. Oh, well. The least he could do was steer her in the right direction.

8

Chris heard the front door and knew another Brown had arrived. It never ceased to amaze him that nearly every waking minute of his day was spent with his wife, Jane. Since college, they had spent most of their lives together. Their day started with a shower, sometimes together. Breakfast was light while CNN would provide the background for toast and their first cup of coffee every morning. Transportation to work was done separately, for a case could demand that one or both of them be in a different location.

Chris caught what he thought was a glimpse of Jane walking past his office. She had the blue dress on that she had lain out on the bed that morning. He remembered that he wanted to help her with the zipper but that sometimes led to delays. After fifteen years he still loved those delays.

Chris yelled, "I wanted to help you with the zipper on that blue dress this morning, love."

"I don't think my husband would have liked that, Mr. Brown."

The reply caused Chris's head to turn quickly toward the door. To his surprise he saw their secretary, Patty, standing in the doorway of his office. "I'm sorry, Patty. ....that blue dress," Chris stumbled over his words.

"That's alright, Mr. Brown," Patty said with a smile. Chris started blushing which made Patty laugh even more.

At that point the front door opened again. This time Jane Brown entered. As Jane took off her coat Patty started laughing again. Jane asked Patty what was so funny. "I think I will let Mr. Brown answer that question. Nice dress."

Chris called out to Jane, "Do you have a second, love?"

"Sure, what's up?" Jane replied.

"I got a call from one of your old classmates' wives this morning," Chris began.

"Who?" Jane asked.

"Marie Al Fozie."

"Really, how is she doing? How is the Al Fozie family?"

"That, I am not sure of but it sounds like husband and wife problems," he said, sadly.

"Did you tell her we don't handle that sort of thing?"

"I think she knows that. I guess she just needs some advice on which way to turn."

"So, how are you going to handle this?" Jane showed her concern.

"I told her to stop in tomorrow morning at nine. Perhaps we can steer her in the right direction."

"What do you mean, we?" Jane said.

"I get the point," Chris replied.

Jane tried to change the subject; "So why was Patty laughing?" After he explained, he listened to both Jane and Patty laugh at him.

TUESDAY (ELEC)

The door to Brown and Brown opened promptly at nine o'clock. Marie Al Fozie entered. Since Chris was the only one in the office he continued to study the file in front of him. Most of the time he would hear something like, 'hello honey, it's just me' but after yesterday morning's blue dress incident he was not about to greet anyone passing by his office door.

Like yesterday he was startled to hear a voice he was not ready for. "Hi Chris," spoke a woman's voice. Chris turned to find Marie Al Fozie standing in the doorway. He rose to his feet and walked to Marie.

"How are you Marie? I'm sorry, I thought it was Jane." Chris offered Marie his hand. "Please sit down. I told Jane you had called and she can't wait to see you. She should be here any minute. Can I offer you coffee or tea? The coffee is ready; tea will take a bit longer." Marie chose coffee. "Would you like cream and sugar?" Chris offered. "Black and one sugar, please," Marie said. Chris placed the coffee in front of Marie and sat down.

Feeling a bit uncomfortable, Chris led off with, "How are you? How are Fozi and your sport model?" Chris was referring to Marie's daughter whose name was also Marie. Their daughter was about seven as Chris remembered. Instead of an answer Marie instantly broke out in tears. Clients frequently react this way but it is usually when they hear how much time the plea bargain was going to get them or the fact that they were going to do no time at all. Kleenex, where are they? Handing Marie a Kleenex, Chris started again, "What's going on kid? Please, what's wrong?"

Marie attempted to gather herself up but the tears kept coming. Chris got up and walked behind her chair. Putting his hands on Marie's shoulders Chris began to massage. "Marie, talk to me. We can get through this. Come on." Just then Jane entered the room, "Honestly Chris, yesterday I am greeted with laughter, this morning tears." Chris stood there dumbfounded, "I, I, I'm sure glad to see you." Marie jumped up at the appearance of Jane Brown and ran to her. The sobbing got worse. Jane comforted Marie and she began to settle down. "Sit down Marie. What is the problem, Chris?" "I haven't gotten that far yet," was Chris's reply.

Once again Marie began to gather herself together. The name Fozi suddenly came from her lips, "Fozi is gone. Fozi left me. Fozi left me, he's gone, he's gone." Chris could handle this; it happens all the time. "He took Marie, he took Marie," she went on. Suddenly Chris had a problem. "What do you mean he took Marie? He moved out? He left the state? What are you saying?" "He's gone," Marie explained, "I think he left the country." Chris said, "When?" Jane stood there and said nothing. Jane could not believe what she'd heard. "How do you know he left the country? How long have they been gone?" continued Chris. "They have been gone for four days," she cried.

"Why didn't you tell me this yesterday?" "I can't tell the police," Marie said as if Chris hadn't spoken. "You don't understand how he thinks. I couldn't tell you on the phone. Please help me. I don't know where to turn or who to turn to." Custody was a huge problem but typically, the mother was where all things started. Both Jane and Chris were speechless for a time and then Jane broke the silence, "Tell us why you think Fozi left the country with Marie. Tell us everything."

"I had a teacher's conference scheduled for last Saturday and Sunday. I don't like weekend conferences but it happens. Fozi had the weekend all planned out...the zoo, the movies. I got home Sunday night and they were not home. I was dead tired so after I cleaned up I went to bed.

"It was eight o'clock when I laid down. I was very tired. The next thing I know it was six-thirty Monday morning. I could not believe I'd slept through the night. Then I noticed that Fozi's bed had not been slept in. We have twin beds," she said reluctantly; "that's how Fozi likes it. I ran to Marie's room and she was gone as well. Her bed was still made. I know he has taken my baby, I know he has."

"We can't be sure of that, Marie," Chris said. "Why didn't you call the police? Have you checked with any friends?"

"He took my baby, he took my baby!" her voice got louder.

"Have you guys been having problems?" Jane asked.

Marie answered, "No, everything has been fine."

"I just don't understand how you can think he left the country," interrupted Chris.

"Around seven o'clock that morning the phone rang," Marie said.

"And?" Chris waited.

"It was the airport police. They said my car had been hit by a taxi in the long-term lot where it was parked."

"Tell us what happened next, Marie?" Jane tried to keep Marie focused.

"I think I fainted," she answered

"You think you fainted?"

"Well, I woke up on the bedroom floor. I must have fainted and fallen against the bedpost."

Marie raised her sleeve to expose a large bruise on her right arm.

"Marie, you have to call the police." Chris reached for the phone. He picked up the receiver and began to dial. Marie jumped to her feet and grabbed the phone from Chris. "You can't let them know what is going on," Marie pleaded. "Chris, you don't understand. Please don't call the police."

"Marie, if you want help you have to let the police in on this."

"No Chris," she argued, "don't you know anybody that can help me? No police. I know you deal with clients from all over the world. You must know someone. You told Fozie you handled some business in Saudi Arabia. You must know someone."

"Marie that was five years ago for a minor acquisition case," Chris looked at her hopelessly.

Marie continued, "Please, Chris, please."

Jane jumped in, "Chris, can I talk to you in my office?"

Marie looked up at Jane, "Please Jane, please Jane, help me in this. You're a mother. Please."

Chris followed Jane into her office. He closed the door as Jane turned around. "Jane, have you lost it? We have to call the police. This is not a Sally Field movie."

"That's not funny!" Jane shot back. "There must be someone we can call for some advice or help. Please try."

"You're killing me, love," Chris sounded defeated.

"I know, Chris, but this is her daughter we're talking about."

"Ok," Chris replied, "I will make a few calls. "

"Thank you, Chris."

"Wait," Chris added. "If I can't come up with anything by tonight, we go to the police." Jane hugged Chris and smiled.

"Thank you, dear," she whispered in his ear.

Chris and Jane returned to Chris's office. Marie jumped up and ran to Jane.
"Chris is going to make some calls, Marie," Jane added, "but if we don't have any luck you must notify the police."

"Alright," Marie started to tear again. "If we can't get help I will do whatever you say."

After that Chris told Marie to go home and wait for his call. He reassured her, "One way or another we will get Marie back to the house." Marie had a look of relief as she walked out of Chris Brown's office with Jane. Chris had a look of dismay on his face.

EARLY TUESDAY EVENING

Chris sat in his study sipping a Cabernet Sauvignon while Peter Jennings did his version of the evening news in the background. The situation with Marie replayed over and over in his mind. A commercial ended that warned you to call your doctor if your erection lasted more than four hours. Chris laughed at the thought of a four-hour woody. Peter Jennings returned to the screen. He led off with a piece on Saudi Arabia. Expatriates and their role in the Arab oil industry was the subject. Chris thought to himself, that's exactly what I need, someone who was employed in the Kingdom. I'd simply give them a ring, send them a plane ticket for little Marie, who they would put on a plane bound for New York, and it's a happy ending. So much for daydreams.

However, the next thought that Chris had made sense. Steve Roach, a childhood friend, was employed by the U.S. Consular Office. Who better would know about expatriates in the Kingdom? Chris flipped his address cards to R; first Richie, then Raven, finally Roach. Chris dwelt on the fact that he had not called Steve in some time; old friends should be called to say hello. He hated the fact that after so much time, he was looking for help. Oh well, Steve will understand.

As adolescents Chris followed Steve around and life was great. They would sneak into the drive- in movies in the summer. Then there was the driving range. Bill Dauber would give the boys five cents a ball for every golf ball they returned to him. Now the deal was that the balls had to be retrieved from the other side of the highway. Steve figured out that there were more balls to be had at the seventy-five yard mark. About nine o'clock at night the boys would cross the highway, crawl under the fence, and proceed onto the driving range. Chris remembered how he felt like Audie Murphy in "To Hell and Back." They would crawl on their bellies and the golf balls would whiz by. Once in a great while one of them would get hit. Chris thought about the term, 'in coming,' which was made famous in movies about war. No one ever got hurt badly, only bruised. Bill D. paid up to three dollars a day for the balls that the boys would turn in. Chris wondered if Bill D. ever knew what was going on. In all fairness they would search for balls on the other side of the street. During the day they would run around in the field across the street and now and then yell, "I got one."

Steve was three years older than Chris so when Steve started taking flying lessons at the local grass field airport, Chris did, too. Chris prided himself in knowing that, although he could not fly without an instructor like Steve, the instructor would let him do all the flying and just sit there. In those days it cost four dollars and fifty cents for a half hour of instruction. Ah, the good old days.

After the second ring Chris heard the voice of his old friend, "Hello?"

Chris started with, "Is this Steve Roach?"

Steve replied, "Yes."

"This is officer Williams of the Newburgh City Police. Am I correct in assuming this is the same Steve Roach that grew up in Newburgh?" Chris was fighting the laughter.

Steve replied, "I did, sir."

"I'm investigating an old case concerning the theft of golf balls from a driving range near your home." Steve picked up on the fact that he was being had and he knew who was doing the job on him.

Steve blurted into the phone, "It wasn't me, sir, I swear, it was not me. It was Chris Brown. He made me do it! He made me do it!"

Chris started laughing, "You dick! You would throw me under a bus like that?"

Steve laughed, "It's a question of survival, pal."

"How the hell are you?" Steve questioned.

"I'm good, Steve. And how are you?" Chris sounded relieved.

"Can't complain, brother. What's up?"

"Let me start with how good it is to hear your voice. I'm sorry it's been so long since my last call. How is Carole?"

"She's great," Steve replied, "how about Jane?"

"She is fine, thank you," Chris said.

Steve's next question was, "Is everything else OK?"

"For the most part," Chris replied.

"I don't like the sound of that," Steve said. "Lay it on me."

Chris told Steve about Marie Al Fozie.

Steve was sympathetic and told Chris that this was not uncommon as of late. "I know of at least five cases like this."

"Who do you go to for help in these cases?" Chris asked.

"The law," was Steve's reply.

"Who do you go to besides the law?" Chris asked again.

"What are you asking me, partner?" Steve decided to cut to the chase.

"In your business you know a lot of people in the Kingdom of Saudi Arabia," Chris started.

"I know who applies for visas to enter into the Kingdom but that information is not for sale. You know all this, Chris.

"I know, but Jane and I are desperate to help Marie somehow. I told her I wanted her to contact the police but she is completely against that."

"What you want is someone in the Kingdom to just put the kid on a plane for New York?" Steve said dubiously.

"That's it!" Chris replied.

"Forget it, Chris!" Steve said.

"What about those expatriates who work in the Kingdom? How would one go about finding one of them?" Chris said.

"Have you ever heard of FISA?" Steve asked Chris.

"I'm not too sure I know exactly what they do," Chris said.

"Well let me tell you something, little buddy. Anyone who leaves the States for any reason makes their list. You need to talk to someone there."

"You don't happen to have a contact with them, do you?" Chris probed.

"I do, and yes, I will make a call. I'm not going to promise anything so don't get excited."

"Steve, you are the best. I promise I won't tell anyone about the golf balls or the movies you made me sneak into." Chris knew this was the biggest favor he had ever asked his friend.

"Up yours, Chris. Remember when I finally got a job at the drive-in? I used to let you come in under the screen by the kiddy rides. I could tell the law about that, too."

"Mum's the word," Chris said thankfully.

"Give me an hour or so and I'll see if I can get you a number or name," Steve said as he hung up the phone.

TUESDAY EVENING, 10 P.M.

Chris had been working on a file for about two hours when the phone rang. As the ringing continued, he raced to finish the paragraph. It was on its fourth ring by the time he could answer, "Brown residence." "May I speak with Chris Brown," said an unfamiliar voice.

"Speaking," Chris replied, as he scanned his memory to place the voice on the other end.

"My name is Pat Henneberry and it seems we have a mutual friend in Steve Roach," the man responded.

Chris was suddenly taken aback. He had gotten so wrapped up in the file he was working on that the call to Steve had slipped his mind. "Ah, yes, Steve. Thank you for getting back to me so quickly, Mr. Henneberry."

"Steve informed me of your client's problem, Chris. What exactly are you looking for?"

"Well, to start with Mr. Henneberry…."

"Call me Pat," he interrupted, "and I shall call you Chris."

"Well Pat, I have to tell you that Marie Al Fozie is not a client; she is an acquaintance. My wife and I merely are trying to give her some direction," confessed Chris.

"Have you thought of the police?" asked Pat.

"Honestly, the mere mention of police and she panics," Chris replied.

"So you are trying to find her someone in the Kingdom who she can call? Does she think that they can just pick up her daughter and send her home on the next flight to the States?" Pat's voice became hesitant, which made Chris question why everyone, including himself, thought it was that easy…just find little Marie and put her on the next plane home.

Chris paused for a moment, "I guess what we are looking for is a person that fits that description, Pat."

"My office is not in a position to help you out with names in this line of work, although we do track expats and their current locations."

"Is there anyone you can recommend, Pat?" Chris didn't care how desperate he sounded.

Pat's next question made Chris nervous, "This conversation is not being recorded, right?"

"No, Pat, this is strictly off the record."

"Do you have a FAX machine?" Pat said hesitantly.

"Yes we do," replied Chris.

"Chris, you should get a FAX in about an hour. This FAX may or may not help you. From it you will see how persons are cross referenced. Check it out and all I can say is, 'Good luck'."

As the words, thank you, began to roll off Chris Brown's lips the phone went dead. Chris sat there thinking, "What have I gotten myself into now?"

TUESDAY EVENING, 11:05 P.M.

For forty-five minutes Chris Brown sat at his desk watching the phone, not bothering to work on his clients' files. He wanted to call it a day. Jane was in bed already. What have I gotten myself into, was all he could think of. Suddenly the phone rang. Chris jumped. Why should he be so nervous? It was the FAX number he had given Pat Henneberry. He had once heard about a fellow that was so nervous he could thread a Singer sewing machine when it was running. He felt like that guy. Chris watched as the FAX machine did its thing and the sheet of paper presented itself. Pick up the paper, fool, was all he thought. Go on, pick up the paper. Finally he made the move. He placed the sheet of paper on the desk in front of him. Either the time of day or his nerves made the paper appear blurry. As he began to focus, a list of agencies appeared. Chris had heard of this kind of list before, but had never actually seen it. It appeared to be a list of 'persons of interest' each government agency was keeping their eye on.

U.S. Dept. of Passports
U.S. Coast Guard
Ship Documentation Office
NYS Dept. Of Registration
Intercontinental Flight Records Office
U.S. Customs Office
Epirp Registration Office
Ham Radio Registration Office
U.S. Embassy, KSA
National Buoy Data System
WeatherImages.Com
Overseas Employment Visa, Issued from Houston, Texas
.

After skimming the page he realized that next to each agency, one name kept popping up, Michael NMN Murphy. He made a mental note of that and the fact that it covered a period of ten years. It also showed that a new passport had been issued this past January for this Mr. Murphy. Glancing at his watch Chris realized it was long past midnight. He thought to himself, "I can't do this anymore." All he could think of was his pillow waiting for him in bed. "Tomorrow is another day."

WEDNESDAY AT HOME

Chris Brown woke up to the alarm clock's ring. Jane lay still. This was a game she played each morning. Chris rolled over against his wife and gently kissed her on the shoulder, her left shoulder. "Good morning, love." Jane rolled over and gave her husband a big hug. "Good morning," followed the hug. As usual Chris got up and started the shower. Jane liked to step into the shower as if it were automatic.

"What happened to you last night, Chris? I was awake until after eleven," Jane said.

"I know, love, and I meant to get to bed early. This thing with Marie Al Fozie is getting complicated."

"In what way?" Jane questioned. Jane handed Chris the soap and asked him to do her back.

"I'll wash anything you want, love," Chris replied.

"Never mind, pal, you had your chance last night and you blew it."

Chris looked at Jane and simply replied, "Damn!"

At breakfast Jane asked Chris exactly what was going on with Marie. Chris told Jane about the two calls and the Fax. "What's next, Chris?" she responded.

"I'm not sure, love."

"Who is Michael Murphy?" Jane asked. "What does he do?"

"He is a Journeyman Wireman," Chris answered.

"What is a Journeyman Wireman?" Jane pursued.

"I'm not sure yet," was Chris's reply.

"Where does he live?"

"Now that is the good news," Chris seemed more positive. "He makes his home about forty miles from here…a town between Rhinebeck and Albany."

"What is his connection? Where does he come into the picture?"

"Michael Murphy happens to be employed in Saudi Arabia. He works as an electrical inspector for an oil company," was all Chris knew.

"So how do you go about contacting him?"

Chris looked at Jane for a moment, "Wait a minute, love, how far are we going to take this?"

"Well, we said we would help her," she argued.

Again Chris looked at Jane, "Do you realize what we are getting ourselves involved in, Jane? This fellow Murphy, do you think he will just drop everything and help Marie? We don't even know where her daughter is."

"Marie said she was in Dhahran."

"So we find this fellow Murphy. We tell him our problem, Marie's problem. Do you think he will just pick up little Marie and put her on the next plane out?" Chris thought to himself: there it is again and so simple.

"Where is Mr. Murphy now?" Jane asked.

"I don't know. All I know is this guy Murphy gets around. For God's sake I don't even understand his job description. He could be anywhere." Chris waved his hands in the air.

"Do you know his address here?"

"Yes."

"Can you call him?" It seemed like work getting this out of Chris.

"Jane, please. I need time to think about this. I want to call Steve Roach back. I have no answers. Perhaps he can give me some ideas. I will call Marie when I get to the office, although I don't know what I'll tell her." Chris was already sorry for getting involved.

"Tell her to call the police," Jane was second guessing this decision as well.

"Right!" Chris said.

Jane looked Chris straight in the eyes. "Chris, we told her we would do what we could. But if we pursue this we are getting others involved."

"Yes, we have already gotten two people involved and Murphy would make three." Chris got up from the table. He gave Jane a peck on the cheek and started for the door.

"Don't forget the awards dinner tonight," Jane said. "Seven o'clock."

"No problem. I'll see you at the office." Chris got into his car, inserted the ignition key, then caught himself staring at the windshield. I thought that this week was going to be a cakewalk. The term foreign intrigue entered his mind...damn!

WEDNESDAY AT THE OFFICE

As Chris drove to the office a thousand thoughts were on his mind. How would he find Murphy? Was he in the States or out of the country? Would he laugh at me? What kind of a person was Murphy? What the fuck is a Journeyman Wireman? Chris reached down for his travel mug and his hand closed around air. Damn! In the middle of all this he had forgotten his coffee. His next thought was not good. I hope this is not an indication of things to come.

With no coffee and his mind racing, Chris pulled into the parking lot and immediately got out of his car. As often happened he was the first one there. After checking his calendar he picked up the phone to call Marie Al Fozie. She answered on the first ring.

"Hello?" said a soft voice.

"Hello, Marie, it's Chris Brown."

"Oh, Chris! Thank you for calling me back. What can I do? Can anyone help me?"

"Marie, I made a call to an old friend of mine last night," Chris began.

"What did he say? Will he help me?"

"He suggested you call the police," he said nervously.
She paused in disappointment, "No, I can't. I can't!" Marie began to sob.

"Marie," he said, "he knows of at least five other cases like this."

"I want my daughter back; he doesn't understand."

"He does, Marie, we all do," Chris knew he didn't fully understand, but this was the speech he had practiced on many of his clients. Sometimes he didn't even realize what he was saying until after it was said. By then, it was always too late to take it back.

"Who will help me, Chris?"

Reluctantly Chris spit out, "I have a name, a man who works in Saudi Arabia."

"Will he help me?" she cried.

"Marie, all I have is a name," Chris went on, "I haven't attempted to get in contact with him yet. I wanted to call you before I do anything else. Are you sure you want to do this without the police?"

"I told you Chris, if there is any other way I want to try first."

Chris thought for a minute, "I need some time to figure this thing out Marie. It may take a day or so to find this guy I've been telling you about. You know, he may think I'm a nut."

"Oh, Chris, thank you! Thank you!"

"Have you heard anything since Monday, Marie?"

"No, not a word."

"Did you go to school?" Chris tried changing the subject.

"Yes. If I didn't have my class I would go crazy."

"Ok, Marie, I'll try to get back to you by Thursday."

"Thank you, Chris, thank you, thank you!" is all she could utter.

"Marie, please don't get your hopes up. I'm still not sure of how to get this going."

"You'll do it, Chris, I know you will," she said with confidence.

"I will try. Until Thursday, goodbye."

"Goodbye, Chris and thank you again."

Chris hung up the phone, "Damn!" he thought.

WEDNESDAY, 9 A.M.

Once again Chris caught himself staring into space as the outer office door opened. "Good morning, Mr. Brown" said a familiar voice.

"Good morning, Patty," Chris replied. Almost immediately the front door opened again. This time he heard the voice of his wife greet Patty and now the team was complete. As Jane and Patty went over Jane's schedule, Chris attempted to figure his next move for Marie Al Fozie. What the hell…call Michael Murphy!. His address was all Chris needed to get his telephone number. What if it was unlisted? Could he get lucky and in fact find this fellow?.

Chris wrote the Murphy address down. The last thing he wanted to do was fumble around when the operator requested the address. He dialed 845-555-1212. When the operator came on and requested, "What city?" Chris replied, "Tivoli." "The party you are calling?" Chris quickly responded, "Murphy, Michael Murphy, at 93 Bellmore Drive." After a "Thank you," and a slight pause, a recording followed, "The number you have requested is 845-475-4709."

Chris hung up and wrote down the number immediately. My God, he does exist, he thought. Don't stop now. Dial the number, get on with it. How the hell do I start the conversation if he answers? What if I get an answering machine?

Finally, Chris found his fingers pushing buttons. Why was this so hard to do? One ring, two rings, three rings, "Hello!" A second time Chris heard the voice of a woman, "Hello?" she said. Suddenly the line went dead. Damn! She must have thought I was a salesman or something. Chris felt rather dumb. As he dialed the number for the second time he felt nervous. One ring, two rings, "Hello?" she sounded annoyed this time.

Chris replied, "Good morning. Is this the Murphy residence?"

"Yes," was the reply, the woman's voice being the same one who had answered the first time.

"My name is Chris Brown and I would like to speak to Michael Murphy, please."

"What is this about, Mr. Brown?" the voice said.

He continued, "It concerns his overseas employment."

"Well, Mr. Brown, I wish I could help you but at this time Mike is somewhere between New York City and Bermuda. Is it important, Mr. Brown?"

Chris thought for a split second and fired back, "Nothing that can't wait a little while longer." He didn't want it to sound like a life or death matter. "When do you think you will hear from Mr. Murphy next? Is this Mrs. Murphy?"

"Mike should be in Bermuda on Saturday or Sunday, and yes, this is his wife. Actually, I am flying down to be with him on Monday. Does this have to do with work, Mr. Brown? You're not going to send him back to Saudi Arabia, are you?"

"No, Mrs. Murphy. That's not it at all." To make things a bit lighter Chris asked Mrs. Murphy how her husband got to go on a cruise without his wife. Mrs. Murphy laughed and told Chris that Mike was not on the QE II. Mike was sailing his own boat to Bermuda.

"His own boat?" Chris replied.

"Yes, we have a thirty-foot sailing ketch," Mrs. Brown boasted.

Since Chris knew a little about sailing and this news interested him, he remarked, "He must be a good sailor to make a trip like that."

"I sure hope so," was Mrs. Murphy's reply. "Do you want to leave a number that I can give Mike next Monday?" Chris thought for a second and asked if there were a number he could call them at in Bermuda.

"Once I get there we will be staying at the Rosdon in Hamilton. Why don't you give us a call on Tuesday around four-thirty in the afternoon, as we're always there for high tea."

"If you don't mind I will do that, Mrs. Murphy," Chris said. "Are you sure that will be alright? You are on holiday."

"No problem, Mr. Brown, no problem at all," she said with ease. Chris thanked Mrs. Murphy for her time and wished her a great trip. Mrs. Murphy gave Chris the hotel number and assured him that Mike would get the message.

Given that it was Wednesday Chris thought he better give Marie a ring. Now he had five more days to wonder how Michael Murphy would react to his call. Sailing to Bermuda from New York in a thirty- foot boat.... Chris liked this guy already.

Chris dialed Marie Al Fozie and, as before, the phone rang only once.

"Hello?" Marie said.

"Hi, Marie, it's Chris."

"Oh, Chris, I forgot my classroom key and had to come back from the car. What timing." Marie seemed out of breath.

"I have some bad news, Marie," Chris went on. "The person I need to speak to is not available until Tuesday."

"That's alright, Chris; I can wait a little longer. 'Bad news would've been if he had refused to help."

"So I will call you next Wednesday. Are you going to be alright Marie?" Chris was sincere.

"Yes, Chris, I'll be fine," Marie muttered out. "And, Chris, thank you again."

Just then Patty walked into Chris's office with a folder in her hand. Seeing Patty helped get his mind back on the normal routine. "You have to be in court at eleven, Mr. Brown, the Smith case," she reminded him.

"Yes, Patty, and I can't wait. Today should be the end of this file," as he reasoned that at least he could put some things behind him.

WEDNESDAY, 1200 HRS: 165 Miles Southeast of New York, Atlantic Ocean

The sailing ketch, Rag Doll, was on a compass heading of 151 degrees. The self-steering system was working in concert with the prevailing wind. However, the skipper was not doing so well. As he hung over the side of his trusty little vessel for what seemed like an eternity, nothing came up. God, I hate sea sickness, was his only thought. For the last twenty-four hours this had been an hourly ritual. Surely it had to stop. He remembered the last passage to Bermuda. All on board had suffered with sea sickness, save one. Eventually Mike, Art, and Al got over it. The fourth member had shared his patches with them.

This time Michael Murphy was attempting the journey on his own. This would be the final test before attempting to cross the Atlantic. For some reason he had forgotten this part. The part where the sickness seems like it will never end. He had the same thought during the night when Rag Doll rolled off a wave. He was thrown against a bulkhead. His first thought was, I forgot about this part. Upon reaching Bermuda in '02 his body was black and blue from top to bottom; the bottom was really bad.

His trip down the Hudson River was a nightmare. From Beacon to the George Washington Bridge he had taken the wind on the nose. At West Point where the river bends the wind bent with it. As the tide was going out, the wind increased from the south. The water was confused and Rag Doll rocked and rolled. Upon reaching the GW Bridge Michael pulled in close to the west shore and dropped the hook. After a fourteen hour run from north of Beacon, he had had enough.

Once he was sure the hook was set, Michael went below. The Palisades seemed to shelter Rag Doll from the wind. This was a regular stopping point for him. With all the beautiful spots in the world to anchor, the Palisades was high on the list. There is something about getting up in the morning and having these steep cliffs greet you. Sleep came quickly.

The morning of June 14 came quickly. Michael had no alarm clock set since he could never sleep past 0700 anyway. As he remembered, the Palisades were a lovely site. The Hudson River as well as the wind had done an about-face. He couldn't believe he was in the same latitude. After a light breakfast, Rag Doll was on her way to the Verrazano Bridge and open seas. There would be one stop at Liberty Landing for fuel. His trip down the Hudson had been done mostly with the motor. It's not good to leave for a seven-hundred mile trip with empty fuel tanks. After refueling Michael set up his steering system and rigged the sails. He did manage to sneak in one last walk to a New York deli from Liberty Landing. In all his travels Michael held that New York City was the only place to get a good hard roll.

Finally it was time. Cast off. Curtain, lights, all props and costumes ready. Everything came down to this moment. He was thankful that his wife and children were not there. At fifty-nine Michael Murphy found goodbyes very hard to handle. There had been many times when sunglasses had to be worn to hide tears.

It's amazing how far it is from Liberty Landing to the Verrazano Bridge. As he left the Statue of Liberty to starboard it seemed to take forever. Rag Doll finally cleared New York Harbor. After setting sails and shutting down the engine, Michael set about on a heading of 151 degrees. What luck…for the prevailing winds were favorable. Seven days from then, Michael hoped to be checking into customs at St. Georges, Bermuda.

The first night was rough. The second day the sea sickness set in and lingered until now, Wednesday at noon. Next came the Gulf Stream. Lord, let me be well by then. As near as he could figure he had done better than seventy-five miles a day. Five-hundred and fifty miles to go! If he could squeeze out one-hundred miles a day life would be so much better. Patience…he had to be patient. At night he would reduce sails before going below, for the winds seemed to pick up. Presently he was running under a full main sail and a 150 headsail. He had yet to hoist the mizzen. When Rag Doll was making better than eight knots he left the mizzen down. The knowledge that his wife would be in Bermuda Monday afternoon kept constant on his mind and he knew that seventy-five miles a day was not going to cut it.

Rag Doll was an Auxiliary Ketch. She was no spring chicken but she was designed by Carl Alberg, who was to sailboats what Frank Lloyd Wright was to architecture. Rag Doll was a traditional hull made for ocean crossings; she could best be described as a stout little boat. There were times when she made Michael Murphy feel like John D. Rockefeller.

TUESDAY, JUNE 21 - 1630 HOURS

Chris Brown reached for the telephone on his desk. The time had finally come to call Bermuda. Most of the week had been great with the exception of this very moment. So much seemed to hinge on this call and yet he was plagued with uncertainty. Mrs. Murphy was very kind when he spoke to her. On the question of sending her husband back to the Middle East, he had lied to her or at least not told her the facts.

The Rosden Hotel was located in Hamilton, Bermuda. Within ten minutes walking time one could be at the famous Bird Cage. This was the scene pictured on postcards sent around the world by the thousands. Cruise ships kept the streets loaded with tourists spending the Yankee dollar. Since the cruise ships weren't allowed to be in port on the weekends, the natives did get a break.

High tea at the Rosden was in full swing. Couples milled about the porch munching on sandwich bits and pastry. Life for all concerned was as good as it gets! Bermuda has a way of making people feel like they were having a taste of paradise.

Joan Murphy sat alone on the porch of the Rosden Hotel. She was the only person who seemed preoccupied with a serious thought. Hotel guests greeted her as they passed by and she would smile. One could see that Joan Murphy had something on her mind.

Suddenly the hotel manager appeared at Joan Murphy's table. Mrs. Murphy stood up upon seeing her. "He's here, finally?"

"No, Mrs. Murphy. You have a call from the States."

"No, what?" Michael Murphy was two days overdue. Joan Murphy was used to things going wrong when sailing was involved. Michael always told her that you could only count on the day you were going to leave a port. As far as when you may get to your destination, that was always a crap shoot.

"Your call is from a Mr. Brown," continued the manager.

Mr. Brown? A Mr. Brown? Joan Murphy was at a loss.

"Do you want the call in your room, Mrs. Murphy?" pursued the manager.

"No, I will take it at the desk" replied Joan.

On the way to the lobby the light finally went on. Mr. Brown. She remembered that he had called right after her husband left for Bermuda. She had told him to call on the following Tuesday and this was it.

"Hello, Mr. Brown, it's Joan Murphy."

"Hello, Mrs. Murphy. How are things in Bermuda? How was Mr. Murphy's passage?"

"Well, Mr. Brown, I wish I had good news for you. Michael is not here yet. I hope to hear from him any minute." Joan hoped that she was right.

Chris Brown was caught off guard. What do you say to a woman in this position? "I'm sure Mr. Murphy is fine," Chris blurted out. How do you comfort someone at a time like this? What do you say? "Is there anything I can do from this end, Mrs. Murphy?" He hoped he could relieve her mind somehow.

"No. I'm sure he will be here soon. These things happen," as she mused, it's certainly not the first time.

"Well, I'd better let you go. You may get a call and I don't want to be taking up your time."

Joan Murphy struggled for her courage and said, "He'll be fine, Mr. Brown. Thank you for your concern. Why don't you call back tomorrow or Thursday?"

"Fine, Mrs. Murphy. I shall call back on Thursday." Mr. Brown then interjected, "Can I leave you my number in case there is something I can do from here?"

"No, that's alright, Mr. Brown. Just give us a call this time on Thursday, when I'm sure Michael will be able to talk to you." Joan hoped with all her heart that her last words were a sure thing.

Chris Brown hung up. He thought he had problems? He began thinking about Marie Al Fozie and Joan Murphy: one without her child, the other without her husband.

TUESDAY, JUNE 21 - 1800 HOURS - Fifty-five miles north of Bermuda

Michael Murphy sat at the helm of Rag Doll. Checking his watch he realized he had been there for twelve hours. As tired as he felt, he knew the journey was nearly over. That thought alone drove him on.

Approximately thirteen hours earlier Michael had gotten up after six hours sleep. After checking the steering system, the compass, and the true wind direction he was ready for a bite to eat. Water and a breakfast bar would start the day. As he opened the breakfast bar he thought about tomorrow's meal around this time…eggs and bacon with toast and coffee, lots of bacon and real coffee.

Suddenly Rag Doll began to veer off to the east. Michael checked the wind indicator atop the mast. Next he checked the sails. Rag Doll continued to veer east. Then it hit him. Check the steering circuits. They were in fact, fine. During the passage he had changed them twice due to wear or chafing. What could be wrong? Michael then stood up and checked the stern of Rag Doll. To his dismay he found that his steering system had parted, the lower half was gone. Lost to the sea. This was final. He had a big problem.

Michael released the steering system from the wheel and began to steer manually. As he brought Rag Doll back on course his mind was doing a hundred miles an hour. At that time he was eighty miles north of Bermuda according to his global positioning system. The facts began to fill his mind. All I have to do is man this wheel for the next twenty four or twenty six hours, and I will be home free. All I have to do is not leave this wheel to eat. I must relieve myself while at the wheel. All I have to do is stay awake.

More than thirteen hours had gone by and he was still awake. The global positioning system now indicated fifty miles to go. The wind had changed direction and Michael Murphy had been running on his engine. Before he started the engine he thought about tacking out to the east for a bit and then turning west for his Bermuda approach. The wind direction was so bad that he thought he would have to run to the British Virgin Islands before tacking back for Bermuda. Out of the question! Start the engine and drop the sails. Drive Rag Doll to Bermuda.

By 2200 hours Michael was ready to try and contact Bermuda Harbor Radio. This is what all ships at sea do as they approach Bermuda. Bermuda Harbor Radio wants you to contact them when you are thirty miles out. This is for your safety and theirs. Michael had been told, in no uncertain terms, that the approach of Bermuda from the north was one of the most dangerous landfalls in the world. Michael would start early.

Turning on the VHF proved fruitless. There was no traffic to hear. His first attempt to call Bermuda Harbor Radio was futile. For the next two hours he would broadcast and receive no reply. Exhaustion was setting in and the radio problem bothered him. The thought that perhaps he should purchase a new radio crossed his mind.

Out of the blue and to Michael's surprise, came a signal. It was a weather report and it was from Bermuda Harbor Radio. To Michael's surprise another call came in. It was a Pan Pan. A call to all ships at sea, an alert. Be on the lookout for a thirty-foot ketch. The ketch is white and has a crew of one. The ketch is bound for Bermuda and sailing from New York. Michael listened closely. The next transmission rocked his mind. The ketch goes by the name of Rag Doll. Last radio contact was June 19.

Michael keyed his mike and started his call. Bermuda Harbor Radio, Bermuda Harbor Radio, Bermuda Harbor Radio, this is the sailing ketch Rag Doll, do you read? After five attempts he gave up. They can't hear me, he thought. I must get closer. Then he thought of his wife, Joan. What must be going on in her mind now? If he could stay awake and if the weather held he may be there by six or seven tomorrow morning. Hell, it was less than two hours until tomorrow morning now.

Three hours went by and he had still not been able to contact Bermuda Harbor Radio. The time was 0100 hours. Michael tried again. To his surprise there was a response. "Read you, Rag Doll. Your signal is weak, your signal is weak." Michael proceeded to explain his position and assured them that he was in no danger. He asked if his wife could be contacted at the Rosden Hotel. He was starting to hallucinate. He repeated himself a number of times. Do you read? Do you read?

Eighteen hours at the wheel was starting to take its toll. So close. So close. Five or six hours to go. I can do it. It's almost over. I can do this. Following Bermuda Harbor Radio for his approach gave Michael his second or third wind. Change course, head east. What was that course number? I've got it. Look for the sea buoy. I've got it. I see Bermuda. I can smell flowers; I see the lights. Life is good.

Michael entered St. Georges town cut at 0530. He dropped his hook at 0600. Customs did not open until 0800. He didn't feel tired anymore. Clean up the sails. Cover the sails. Clean the deck of lines. Get the fenders ready for the docks. Quarantine was over in less than two hours. Soon he would see his wife. Life is good!

WEDNESDAY, JUNE 22 - 5:39 A.M.

Marie Al Fozie was still asleep. Her drug-induced sleep was not what she wanted. Marie hated taking pills of any kind. She had not been able to get to sleep since Fozi left with her daughter. In the end she turned to sleeping pills. Whatever gets you through the night, as John Lennon put it. Her mind was always on her daughter, day and night. Even as she slept... it was Marie.

At one point she heard something in the background. The sound, though familiar, would not stop. Suddenly, she sat up! The sound was the doorbell. The clock read 05:39. How long had someone been out there pressing the bell? Who could it be?

Marie got up and grabbed her robe. Running for the door, her mind was racing again. Could it be Marie? Was she home? Marie opened the front door without checking to see who might be there. As she looked out she saw a car pulling away. Who could it have been? Looking down, Marie saw an envelope on the floor. She picked it up and saw that it was addressed to her but had no return address or stamp.

Marie closed the door and opened the envelope. Pulling out the sheet of paper inside she saw what seemed to be instructions. Flight #631, Newburgh, 08:30 a.m.; be there. The note was signed: a friend. She is coming home! Someone has come to her aid. Chris Brown, it must be Chris Brown.

Marie quickly dressed and headed for the airport. By the time she got there it was 07:45. There was no traffic and the parking lot was empty. All she could think of was her daughter's return. Marie checked the flight schedule for incoming planes. There was no flight 631. What now?

Marie went to the only information booth that was open. The attendant checked the flight schedules and could find nothing. Marie felt desperation setting in. Please check again she asked. Again, the answer was negative.

As Marie turned to leave, the attendant called her back. "Perhaps you should check the New York Air National Guard, Miss." That's it, she thought! The Air Guard. They use this field also. Marie got directions to the Air Guard hanger. Thanking the attendant, she left the main lobby.

A short drive to the Air Guard hangar and her car was parked again. It was now 08:15. Soon she would have her baby back. Marie could not get the smile off her face. As she entered the hangar she could not help but notice the lack of security. Marie didn't care. Her daughter was coming home.

She noticed a fork lift operator driving towards the hangar door. He must be getting ready to unload the plane. The operator stopped the fork lift at the entrance. He just sat there as if waiting. Suddenly he began to back up. There came a sound from the machine as it backed up. The signal was a warning for those behind the unit to beware. The buzz was intermittent. The buzz was annoying. Buzz-buzz-buzz-buzz.

Marie sat up. What was going on? Now her head was spinning. The buzz continued. Marie tried to focus. Then reality set in. Marie was in her bed. It was a dream. The buzz was her alarm clock.

Marie began to cry. It was all a dream. There was no flight #631. There was no note left at the door. No ringing doorbell. No daughter to hold and love. Today would be another day without her baby.

She must call Chris Brown. She had to speak to someone.

9:00 A.M - SAME DAY

Two hours and three cups of coffee later Marie reached for her phone. Her fingers punched out seven digits and the ringing began. By the fourth ring Marie was preparing herself for the answering machine. "Good morning, Brown and Brown." Caught by surprise Marie blurted out, "Hello, Chris? Chris, it's Marie."

"Hello, Marie. I had a feeling we would be having a chat today."

"Have you found me any help?"

Chris replied instantly. "My plan for today was to have the answer to that very same question. I have to get back to you, Marie. I am in hopes of speaking to someone about four o'clock this afternoon. As I said, you would be the next call."

Marie for the first time in days felt that there was hope. She paused.

Chris called into the phone, "Marie, Marie are you there?"

Marie answered, "Yes. Yes, I'm here. I shall be at my phone from three-thirty on. Thank you Chris, thank you." With that Marie hung up.

Chris Brown found himself getting caught up in this problem. At this time he was not sure if Michael Murphy had made landfall in Bermuda. And what happens when or if Mrs. Murphy is called to the phone at their hotel? What do I say? Have you got any good news as of yet, Mrs. Murphy? Can we do anything for you from here? There has been nothing on the news and I am sure that is a good thing.

4:06 P.M. - SAME DAY

Chris dialed the number for the Rosden Hotel. The call went through in seconds and he knew it was show time. Chris was thinking. Funny how you can pick up your phone and place a call to Bermuda in seconds. Yet you just try to call your house. Never could get through.

The reception desk answered, "The Rosden Hotel." Chris said hello and asked if he could speak to Mr. Michael Murphy. Mr. Murphy should be at high tea. If there is any problem I will understand. I could call back later. Chris decided to level with the receptionist. "Can you tell me if Mrs. Murphy is OK? Did her husband get there yesterday or today? I certainly would not want to upset her even more."

The receptionist began to laugh. Something instantly told Chris that he was there, safe and sound. "You are the fourth or fifth caller to call for Mr. Murphy. Everyone has been worried and afraid to upset Mrs. Murphy. But let me tell you, Mr. Murphy is fine and by pool side with a spot of tea. Let me get the phone to him."

A mellow hello came in from the phone in Bermuda.

"Hello, Mr. Murphy. I'm sorry to bother you; I know your wife was worried."

Michael Murphy cut in. "It's alright, partner. What's up?"

Chris began with an introduction and then asked how the trip went. He went on about how he didn't know anyone who had ever done something of this nature. "You must be tired?"

Murphy thanked Chris for being so kind and offered, "Perhaps we could sail together some time, when I'm home."

That would be nice Chris thought. A nice sail and I bet this guy has some stories.

Getting down to business, Michael went on, "So what can I do for you, Chris Brown?"

Chris touched on a few fine points with Murphy as Murphy listened intently and said nothing. Chris was nervous; this was not what he did for a living. "I am trying to locate someone who may know someone who may know someone or have a relative in the Kingdom. Through the grapevine, sir, your name came up. I will explain the grapevine later if you don't mind."

"So let me get this straight. You need someone to bring a small child back to the USA for you? Is that it Chris Brown? We both know that nothing can be settled today. If there were something I could do for you, we need to get together in about three weeks. I still have friends in the Kingdom. Who knows?"

Chris thought again. Why has he not told me to call a cop? He talks to me as if he may consider helping. There must be something to him.

"Can I call you in about three weeks, Mr. Murphy? Or would four be better?"

Murphy's reply was simple. "Call in three weeks and find out if that Old Atlantic and Gulf Stream were good to me. I have only one other question for you, Chris Brown."

"What is that, Mr. Murphy?"

"While you were checking out the grapevine did you happen to notice what my balance was on my E-Z Pass?"

Chris Brown laughed. "You got me on that one, Mr. Murphy."

THREE WEEKS LATER

Chris Brown pulled his car into the parking lot and knew he was very late. It was ten o'clock in the morning and his head was badly in need of at least two more Excedrin. The celebration of their Little League victory got out of hand. As it turned out, the parents of the kids wanted to surprise him with an adult party. It crossed his mind that, should they get to this point next season, he was going to stay with pizza and soda and his team.

Entering the office he could see Patty was hard at it on the computer and Jane's door was closed. Jane was with a client and he didn't feel like talking to anyone about anything. Dropping his briefcase to the floor he sat down as fast as he could; now he could hold his head up with his hands. Never again was all he could think of.

Suddenly his office door opened and Patty walked in with a cup of coffee backed up with a bottle of Excedrin.

"I figured you would want this black, no sugar, Chris. You look like, well, you don't look good. Two or three Excedrin?"

"Three please and thank you for not using the S word."

"Did you have a good time, Chris?"

"What I remember was fun."

"Congratulations on your season."

"Thank you, Patty."

Patty left the office and returned to her desk, closing the door behind her. Chris sipped at the coffee and threw down the three Excedrin. Knowing this would take an hour or so to go away, he tried to focus on his desk and calendar. His calendar read July 17th. Reaching for the page, he tore off the 17th and found it hard to focus on the 18th. There was only one line and it looked like the 8 word to him, over and over. Never again, was all he could think of.

As the few words and numbers began to come into focus, his head hurt even more. Call Michael Murphy at his home, 845-454-4079. Finally the day had come to address Marie Al Fozie's problem. Chris Brown was still not sure about this situation, and the way he felt at the time did not help. Marie had waited three weeks for this day. Maybe I should stop feeling sorry for myself and remember that others have real problems. Now he really felt bad.

Dialing the number was easy, as it turned out, and in two rings he heard the voice of Michael Murphy saying hello.

"Mr. Murphy, it's Chris Brown. Can I assume all went well?"

"Yes you can, Chris, and how are you?"

"I've been better, sir, but that's another story."

"How is your friend doing with her problem?"

"No change, Michael. Have you given any more thought to what could be done?"

"Well, I have, Chris, but you know this would take some time. One would have to get into the Kingdom and then do his homework. They would need to know where exactly the husband is making his home. What type of routines he follows? How would the child feel about returning to her Mom? Would a stranger scare the child? He would have to have a fool proof way to convince the child to leave with him, that he was bringing her back to her Mom. I could go on for a long time, Chris. Chris, I think we should all meet and try to come up with some answers."

"How would one get into the country, Michael?"

"As luck would have it, Chris, I have a job offer. You didn't know already? I thought your information source would have told you by now."

Chris could not believe what he was hearing. This fellow was considering doing this himself. He had to meet this guy.

"I can set up a meeting for next week, Michael. How about the 24th, at 10 a.m.?"

"I can do that. In the meantime, I shall accept the job offer and get the ball rolling. If this is not going to happen, I can change my mind and roll the job."

"What do you mean by roll, Michael?"

"I will not take the job, I will tell them I changed my mind."

Michael's next question made Chris suddenly sober.

"Are you sure you want to get involved in this thing, Chris? Can your friend be trusted? This could be an international incident, my friend. This will be an international incident! Something like this has to be done so that you and I will never be connected. I know you have as much to lose as I do."

Fear and excitement came over Chris Brown at the same time. As a tide washes over a beach, he could feel a blush rush over him.

"See you on the 24th, Michael."

MURPHY

The phone call had taken Michael Murphy by surprise although he knew it was due. He had been home for only three days and was still standing on sea legs. The worst time was when he would relieve himself. Anytime he had to stand still he always caught himself swaying back and forth. It usually took about a week to get his land legs back.

The passage from Bermuda went as well as could be expected. His son and son-in law had joined him for the return trip. While Michael's son was an experienced sailor, his son-in-law had never sailed. Lou took to the task like a natural. Once you clear Bermuda waters you go on a port tack for about seven days. Michael's son, whose name was also Michael, found the port tack boring after the third day out. With the loss of the wind-vane steering system someone had to be at the wheel at all times. Murphy set up four-hour shifts knowing that in the end all would be tired. After a shift or watch, the correct thing to do is sleep. It never works out like that as luck would have it. After you unwind and eat something you lose up to two hours.

The weather didn't help either. They spent two days becalmed and two days with super-light breezes. Add those four days to a passage that takes seven days normally and you end up with three tired sailors. Oh, yes, there was that squall in the middle of the fifth night. Then there was the time when a headsail was washed overboard and got caught in the prop. Murphy knew that both his son and Lou were better sailors in the end. Murphy also knew that it would take some time for them to know it.

For the next two days Murphy would work on Rag Doll. She had once again returned her crew home safely and was in need of TLC. Salt water raises hell with anything it touches so a fresh water bath was in order. His son, Michael, and Lou had returned to their normal life on land so the task of cleaning was his. Rag Doll would have to be pulled out of the water and stored on land for what looked like his upcoming absence.

Now, Joan was another story. He had promised her he was done with the Middle East so this might become a serious problem. Under no circumstances could she know about his possible rescue request. For thirty-five years her life had been one adventure after another. She once said that if she was not involved, she was standing by wondering if her husband was safe. Murphy knew that this had to be his last trip if he intended to stay married.

THE KELLYS

Murphy's time on the road had always been connected with two brothers from Connecticut. The Kellys and Murphy met in Utah back in 1976. John Kelly was a married man with three children, all girls. Laurence was single and a twice-decorated war vet, Vietnam. After their chance meeting they seemed to always be together or at least close. Murphy often wondered what life would have been like had he not met the Kellys. Since he was an only child it was like having real live brothers. There was always concern for each other, it seemed.

After Utah their lives were never dull. They worked in ten states and two countries together. From Alaska to Saudi Arabia they worked the largest projects there were. Murphy once asked the Kellys if they realized that every project they had worked on had been on "60 Minutes?" One flop house in Fairbanks that Laurence and Murphy stayed in was even featured on "60 Minutes."

Now he would have to call Laurence and accept the latest job offer. Larry and John were still in the Kingdom. As always, when they knew Murphy was not working, they would be on the phone. And, always, Murphy was grateful. It had been two years since his last tour in the Kingdom which he thought at the time was to be his last. Larry was going to be surprised.

If Murphy was going to pull this possible kidnap off, and in all honesty it was a kidnapping, the Kellys were the guys to have covering his back.

THE MEETING

The morning of July 24 was sunny and warm. Traffic on the way to work was nonexistent for Chris Brown. There was a time when Chris would tell himself that if his day started out this way it would be downhill all the way. Those days were long gone and this day had been on his mind for the last week. The meeting: Michael Murphy, Marie Al Fozie, and yours truly, he was thinking.

Getting to the office early did not help him relax as it usually would have. He found himself walking around the office checking things: the coffee pot, the FAX machine, the copy machine, the mail and finally the floor. That's when it hit him. He was one bundle of nerves. Relax man! Get a hold of yourself. You got yourself into this and you are going to get yourself out.

By nine forty-five he had calmed down some. Jane and Patty had arrived and both were involved in the daily routine. He was hoping Jane would come in and ask if he wanted her present for the meeting. That was not to happen this day. While they both knew that this day was coming, Jane was not going to get involved. Chris had kept her up to date on the progress and all she did was listen, no feedback. He knew that, with Jane, no feedback meant I do not like this.

In the parking lot two strangers pulled in, one directly behind the other. The second car came to a stop as the first car struggled to park...another 4x4 fighting to park in a sports car parking space. After the ordeal was over the second car slid in between two Hondas. Both parties reached the front entrance to Brown and Brown at the same time. As the older man opened the door, he motioned for the young lady to enter. "Thank you, sir." "You're welcome," replied the man.

Patty looked up from her desk to see both parties standing there. "May I help you?" Marie looked toward the man and he motioned for her to go first. "I have an appointment with Mr. Brown at ten o'clock."

"And you are?"

"Oh, I'm sorry, I'm Marie Al Fozie."

Standing nearby, the old timer listened and started putting two and two together. This must be the friend with the problem, he thought.

Patty buzzed Chris and told him Marie was there.

"Go ahead and send her in, Patty," Chris replied, after which Patty directed Marie into Chris's office.

Patty addressed the man, "May I help you, sir?"

"Well, young lady, I think I have the same appointment," was his reply.

Patty looked quite confused. "Excuse me, sir?"

"My name is Michael Murphy and I also have a ten o'clock with Mr. Brown."

What bothered Patty was the fact that neither appointment was on Chris's calendar. Collecting herself, she once again buzzed Chris, while at the same time saying, "One minute, please," to the stranger.

A quick response came from Chris, "Yes, Patty?"

"I'm sorry, but there is a gentleman here to see you named Michael Murphy, and he says his appointment is also for ten o'clock."

"It's OK, Patty, you can send Mr. Murphy in."

"Alright, Chris," a puzzled Patty replied, as she then directed Mr. Murphy toward Chris's office. "Go right in, sir."

As Michael Murphy entered the office, Chris was still shaking Marie's hand. He then turned to Mr. Murphy, saying, "We finally meet." His hand went out to Murphy's and the greeting felt as though they already knew each other.

Chris turned to Marie Al Fozie smiling and said, "Marie, I would like you to meet Michael Murphy. Mr. Murphy is here to give us some guidance."

To Chris' surprise, Marie broke down. The tears must have been there all along just waiting to flow. Murphy felt uncomfortable, as did Chris. Leading Marie to the nearest chair, Chris suggested she sit down while handing her a tissue. He turned to Murphy and moved a chair in his direction, motioning him to sit.

Continuing, Chris asked, "Marie, if you need a minute we can…."

But Marie quickly broke in, "I'm OK. I'm okay, really."

Chris took a seat and looked at both of them. "How do we start this, guys?"

Almost knocking over her chair, Marie jumped up and ran over and grabbed Michael Murphy's hand. "Can you get my baby back, Mr. Murphy? Please, can you help me?"

Murphy immediately got to his feet and guided Marie back to the chair. "Please sit down, Mrs. Al Fozie. Let's all talk about this. We will do what we can but first we have to talk."

Amazingly, Marie calmed down but her eyes looked straight into Murphy's, as if to say, 'this man Murphy is not going to give me any false hope.'

"Have you considered going to the law?" was his next question. "Mothers have rights, you know."

"If I go to the law it will take years. Do you know what her life would be like over there? She has been raised in America and this is where she belongs. Do you know how young girls are treated there?"

Stopping her right there, Murphy responded, "I have a good idea and please understand, I know what you are going through."

"No, you don't, Mr. Murphy. You couldn't possibly understand."

Chris Brown thought it was time to step in. "Marie, please try to relax. Mr. Murphy has some important questions to ask you. Please try to listen carefully to him; he only wants to help you."

Marie slowly sat back from the edge of her chair and tried her best to contain herself, saying, "I'm sorry, Mr. Murphy, for the outburst but as you can imagine, I'm very distraught."

Again Chris broke in. "I'm going to have some coffee sent in unless you guys would rather have tea. Let's relax for a few minutes and collect ourselves."

MEETING AFTER THE BREAK

Chris had requested Patty to bring a pot of coffee into his office. Knowing Patty did not much like playing the role of a waitress, he profusely thanked her. "Just leave the tray, Patty, and I will take care of the rest." Patty left Chris's office, going straight to Jane's.

"Do you have any idea what is going on in Mr. Brown's office, Jane?" said a baffled Patty.

Jane directed Patty to close her door, telling her, "I can't reveal what's up at this time, Patty. Only that Chris is acting as a go-between for the two parties in his office."

"But, I knew nothing of a meeting this morning," Patty said, "and that's unusual."

Jane looked at Patty knowing that she was not used to being left out of the loop. "Unfortunately, I am not at liberty to say any more, Patty, at least not at this time."

In the other room, Chris poured coffee for the three of them. After he sat down he took a deep breath and began. "Mr. Murphy, I know you are aware of Marie's problem. Without bringing the law into the picture, what other course could be taken?"

Murphy looked at both of them thinking: someone needs to get into the Kingdom for one reason or another...the child has to be located and contacted...and most importantly, the child has to trust the contact. Speaking he said, "The child is seven or eight, Mrs. Al Fozie?"

"She will turn eight in two weeks," Marie answered.

"So, she has reached the age of reason, I can assume? said Murphy.

"My daughter is very smart, sir, and that's not just from a mother's perspective."

"But, do you think she has had enough of Middle East life, yet?" Mr. Brown persisted.

"She and I are very close, Mr. Murphy. My husband would have had to convince her that the trip was a surprise or that I would be joining them in a day or so."

Murphy asked Marie if she had any idea where the husband would be making his home. "Will he be living with family or friends?"

"I used to have an address in Dhahran that belonged to his parents, Mr. Murphy. They visited us, but we never traveled there to see them."

"Do you know how many brothers and sisters your husband has?"

"One of each but they make their home in France, not in the Middle East."

"And how many wives did his father take?" That question threw Marie off. "Fozi never said that his father had married more than one woman."

"What company did he work for here?"

"Baltic Oil," Marie said.

"So he knows the oil business then?"

"Why do you ask that, Mr. Murphy?"

"Because it seems to me that a fellow would stay in the field he was trained in, wouldn't you think?"

At this juncture Marie got to her feet and began to pace feverishly back and forth. "I will pay you anything you ask, Mr. Murphy. I have my own money. These questions are making me crazy! I just want my daughter back and I have been waiting for weeks for some help. I can't take this any longer! Tell me you know someone that can help me, tell me that you will help me, tell me something. Do you have any children, Mr. Murphy?"

Murphy answered, "Yes I do, Mrs. Al Fozie." Murphy continued, "Money is not a major factor. If I was to help you by setting up something, the party would be getting paid on both ends: by the company that hires him and by you also. To get my contact into the country could be done in two to three weeks as luck would have it. Have you ever made a DVD, Mrs. Al Fozie?"

Marie answered, "No."

"We have to have a way to convince your daughter that she would be returning to her mom. If you made a DVD with me that I could show her, it might work. Perhaps it could be done at your home, some place that she can relate to. Her favorite doll or bear in your hands. Tell her you are giving it to me for her so that she knows I am her friend."

Chris Brown listened and was amazed. That part might work, he thought. If the child was not happy it might just work.

Murphy asked Mrs. Al Fozie if her husband had ever received mail from the Kingdom. She told him that Fozie and his parents always used e-mail.

"That's too bad," Murphy replied.

Marie asked Murphy if he was going to bring her daughter home to her. If they were going to make this DVD together, did that mean he was going to be the one to help her?

Murphy sat back and once again looked at both of them. "If I doctor up the DVD it could be anyone we wanted it to be. I can do the original and we can take it from there." Marie smiled and looked down for some reason. Murphy glanced at Chris Brown and winked.

Now a smile came to Chris's face. He was thinking the same thing the old man was. Michael Murphy was going to do this himself.

Murphy stood up and took the last sip of his coffee. "Let's make the DVD on Saturday. You put it together, Chris, and call me with a time and address for pick up." His next thought was that cup of coffee. He was going to have to pee on the way home if he didn't go. "May I use your restroom, Chris?"

Marie sat down and took a deep breath. "I don't know how to thank you, Mr. Murphy."

Murphy looked at Marie Al Fozie and smiled, thinking to himself, it's not over yet, kid.

Showing Murphy to the bathroom, Chris remarked, "You're alright, Mr. Murphy." With that, Murphy looked at Chris saying out loud this time, "It's not over yet, kid."

SATURDAY MORNING

Michael Murphy left his home at 5:30 a.m. He had told Joan that he was going to work on their boat, getting it ready to be hauled. Murphy knew that if his wife had any idea of what he was really up to, the shit would hit the fan. It was partly true for he did intend to stop at the Yacht Club and check on Rag Doll. Once the inspection was complete he would be off to Marie Al Fozie's home to make the movie.

Marie got up at 7:00 a.m., excited at the prospect of talking to her daughter, even if it was through a DVD. She had taken her daughter's favorite doll out of her room. Marie had been sleeping in her daughter's room for weeks now, and she had in fact been keeping the doll with her. She thought some might think her crazy but it made her feel better. The meeting had been set up by Chris Brown for ten o'clock and needless-to-say, Marie was on pins and needles.

Chris would leave his home for the meeting at 9:00 a.m. Once again, Jane had not offered to get involved. Since the meeting on the 18th, neither one of them had discussed the subject at all. This was not at all like Jane, and at times he wished the whole thing had never started. The funny part of it was that Marie was Jane's friend, not his. Chris knew that he was the one who had told Marie to come to their office, and it would be he that would make this thing go away.

As luck would have it, Chris's home phone rang just before he was about to leave. To his surprise it was Steve Roach.

"Is that you, Chris?" Chris knew instantly who it was.

"Yes it is, Steve, and how are you?"

"Good, partner," Steve answered.

"I didn't call at a bad time, did I, Chris?"

"No, this is good, Steve, what's up?"

"Your friend Murphy is showing up on my screen again, Chris. Looks as though he is returning to the Kingdom again. You wouldn't know anything about it, would you, Chris?" continued Steve.

Chris answered, no, before he even thought about it. "I did speak to him but all he would say is that my friend should seek help from the law." Chris added that he had spoken to him about a month ago.

"Has your friend contacted anyone for help that you know of?"

"Steve, I had to wash my hands of the whole thing. I don't need an international incident, if you know what I mean."

Steve went on with small talk and all Chris could think of was how he had just lied to a friend. By the time the chat was over he felt like a heel.

"Well, you did the right thing, Chris. You can't fix all the problems of the world. Many children have been taken out of the United States; and believe it or not, some do make it back to their mommas or daddies. Sometimes things fall through the cracks but we do the best we can."

"So, when shall we get together, Steve? How's your calendar?" he went on to say, as much to change the subject as anything.

"Well, I'll have to call you back next week, Chris. First, let me see what Carol has lined up for me."

After hanging up Chris was worried. What if he were to find out about this? Somehow he had to keep this quiet. By the same token he would tell Murphy about the call from Steve. He had to be truthful with Murphy no matter what.

By eleven o'clock the video was underway. Marie had been coached and was assuring her daughter that Mr. Murphy was there to bring her home to her mom. She had done the 'I love and miss you' lines and they came naturally. Marie was holding a rag doll in her hands all through the video. Little Marie had had that doll since birth. Her mother stressed that Annie (the doll) wanted to help Mr. Murphy bring her home and to trust Mr. Murphy, and she would be with her mom in no time. She went on to record that if her daughter didn't want to come home, little Marie was to tell Mr. Murphy and Annie and they would let mom know. But even if she didn't want to come home, she could keep Annie with her.

The last words were making Marie choke inside but this is what Murphy instructed her to say. He told Marie that he would not take the child if she did not want to come.

Marie and Murphy stood together and again Marie assured the child that Murphy was a friend. She handed Annie to Murphy. Murphy took Annie in his hands and smiled. Facing the video machine, Murphy assured the child's mother that Annie was going to be with her daughter as soon as possible.

As Chris ended the video, a torrent of tears started coming down Marie's face. Murphy put Annie into his backpack and then took Marie into his arms. "Be strong, Marie. Be strong and patient." Marie looked at Murphy and a smile came across her face as she said, "I know you will bring my baby home to me. Thank you, Mr. Murphy!"

Murphy returned Marie's smile before starting for the door.

Before Murphy could leave, Chris asked him if he could see him outside.

Murphy looked back saying, "No problem, Chris."

Outside Chris told Murphy about the call from his old friend.

"It's OK, Chris. No one leaves the country that someone does not know about it." But then quickly followed with, "Who does your friend work for, Chris?"

Chris looked at Murphy and wished he could tell him. "I told him that you would not get involved and suggested we contact the law. I told him we had not spoken in a month."

Again Murphy asked Chris who his friend worked for.

"You know that I can't tell you that, Michael."

Again Murphy smiled. "Okay, I understand, Chris."

Chris reached for Murphy's hand. "Good luck Michael Murphy and Godspeed."

"See you in a month or so, Chris."

Murphy climbed into his pickup and drove away.

Chris stood watching as Murphy's truck moved out of sight. This fellow Murphy was one of a kind, he was thinking. For a second he thought it would be fun to go with him and help. His next thought was that he must be crazy!

THE BROWN SHOWDOWN

Chris Brown got back to his house about one o'clock. He couldn't get Murphy off his mind, how could he have a plan already, maybe he didn't have a plan at all. Shooting from the hip was one thing, but seven thousand miles from home. The man was leaving for Saudi Arabia with a DVD and no apparent plan.

Jane was sitting in the kitchen when Chris entered through the back door.

"Hello, love," was the best he could come up with. Jane turned her head toward Chris and said nothing. The seconds felt like minutes and then she started.

"You didn't tell me you were going anywhere this morning, Chris."

"I'm sorry, Jane, but I had to meet with Murphy and Marie at ten o'clock. I didn't think you wanted anything to do with this mess. I mean you haven't shown anything but discontent since day one."

"Maybe so, but I still want to know what the hell is going on; this is bullshit! We have worked too hard to get involved in something that could cost us our practice. WE."

Irritated, Chris interrupted Jane. "What's this 'WE' shit? Marie was your friend. I seem to remember you telling her that we would come up with something. In the end it seems that I am on my own. You made no attempt to sit in at the first meeting during the week. Believe it or not, I was hoping you would join us, kid."

"I was busy," Jane replied. "You didn't tell me there was a meeting planned. Patty didn't know either. Patty was pissed. You know she doesn't like surprises like that."

"Oh, is that right? So Patty is pissed?"

"Yes, that's what I said."

"Well, if she has a problem, I'll discuss it with her on Monday."

"There's a good idea. I can hear it now. Patty, we are planning to kidnap a little girl in Saudi Arabia. Her mom asked us to set it up, and I am sorry I didn't get a chance to let you know. If we need some reservations made in the near future, I will let you know. What's this Murphy like? I mean, you don't even know this man."

Chris looked at Jane and instinctively knew there was nothing he could say that would calm her down. So instead he told her, "I just need time, Jane. This thing is out of my hands already. Murphy doesn't want us, me, involved anymore. I have no idea what he intends to do once he goes back to Saudi Arabia. As it stands now he is armed with only a DVD that we made this morning."

"A what?" Jane asked.

"You heard me right, Jane, a DVD."

Chris went on to explain what had gone on that morning while Jane listened. When Chris was done he just sat there, looking at Jane.

She looked Chris straight in the eyes. "Is that all you have to tell me? What about the part where the child agrees or not. What about the part where he finds the child to start with? What about the getaway?"

Chris knew of only one way to answer, saying, "It's out of my hands, Jane, I don't know."

Jane looked at him and simply shook her head. "You're crazy. Murphy is crazy. Both of you are just plain nuts!"

Chris remembered Murphy's words at that moment. It ain't over yet, kid.

THE MURPHY SHOWDOWN

Michael Murphy arrived home at four o'clock that afternoon. After parking his pickup and unloading boating equipment, he knew it was time to face the music. One thing Murphy never liked was telling Joan he was going on the road again. The road was one thing but the fact that he was going to leave the country again…not good.

Murphy found his wife preparing dinner. The aroma of apples filled the room since she had spent the afternoon baking. What is better than the smell of apple pie filling the house? Two lovely pieces of prime rib sat near the stove which was one of Murphy's favorites. A good old-fashioned meal: steak and potatoes.

"Hello, sugar. It looks and smells as if you've been very busy today."

"Hello," Joan replied. "Well, hello. Where have you been all day and don't tell me the Club."

"Okay, I started out at the Club but then I had to meet with that fellow, Chris Brown."

Joan gave her husband a look. Murphy hated that look. He knew that she knew something was up. Now if he could just keep from smiling as he answered her he might have a chance. Whenever Murphy was nervous due to a question his wife might ask, he would always smile. As soon as the smile was on his face he knew that she knew whatever he was about to say was bullshit.

"Chris Brown was that guy who called you in Bermuda, right?"

"Yes, dear," was all Murphy could come up with, feeble as it was.

"Don't 'Yes, dear, me!' What's going on Mike? Does this have anything to do with the Middle East?"

Now Murphy knew he was at the part where a smile would blow the whole day. The steaks would fly across the kitchen followed by that wonderful apple pie. Suddenly he was glad he could not see any potatoes; they really make a mess.

Keeping a straight face, Murphy began. "This guy Brown wants me to help one of his clients with a problem."

"And the problem is?" as she waited to hear this latest story.

"Do you remember that movie about the child abduction, Joan? I think Sally Field was in it," Murphy added. "It took place in the Middle East or someplace like that."

Getting exasperated, she said, "Can we just cut to the chase, Mike?"

"Hang on, sugar. I didn't say I would do anything yet." The minute he said 'yet' he knew he had made a huge mistake.

"Yet! What exactly do you mean by, 'yet'? You're not going back there, Michael, get that out of your head right now."

"Give me a break. I didn't say I would do that. I told him I would see if I could find someone who could help. Larry Kelly is still there, you know. Why do you always have to jump to conclusions?"

"I jump because I know you, pal. Look me straight in the eyes and tell me you're not thinking about going back there, Mike. When you spoke to Kelly he asked you to come back, right?"

"There was a job offer, I'll admit that."

"That bastard! He knows you promised me you would not go back there. Why does he do that? You're all alike. Don't you want to be here with me? Why do you have to be on the road all the time? And this! When you're not on the road, you're out to sea. I'm supposed to just sit and wait while you have a good ole time. For the love of God, Mike! When you arrived in Bermuda you looked like you had been beaten with a bat. You never know when to quit."

"That was from rough seas, Joan. Sometimes that can happen."

Exploding, Joan said, "Damn you! You were three days late and for all I knew you were dead."

"My radio was the problem there, Joan. If I could have gotten through to you, you know I would have."

"It's all bullshit, Mike! I hate this!" Joan began to cry. She sat down and this was more than Murphy needed.

"I haven't said I was going to do anything, Joan. Please don't get so upset."

"Upset! You don't even have a clue, do you? I'm pissed, Mike, big time. I don't think I can take this any longer."

Murphy tried to temper the situation. "Please, Joan, I told you I haven't committed yet."

"Don't give me that. Yes you have, Mike. You have but you just will not admit it." And with that, Joan left the kitchen and headed to the bedroom. This conversation was over.

THE MURPHY SHOWDOWN, PART TWO

Murphy walked over to the stove. He asked himself if he should do both of the steaks or just one for him. Joan was gone for the rest of the day and there would be no quiet meal tonight. Michael Murphy knew that he would be heading out in a couple of weeks to join the Kellys. Why was it so hard to just tell the truth? The worst part was that he knew that Joan knew the same thing. Why did they always have to fight about shit that they both knew the answer to. She would say that he would never change and he knew she was right.

The answer is one steak. Murphy wrapped the second steak and put it into the fridge. After getting the potatoes ready and boiling them, his steak went on. Murphy didn't like a steak cooked too long, just knock the cowboy off it.

After his quiet meal he watched TV for some time and finished the evening off with a book. Perhaps tomorrow would not be too hard on them; maybe Joan would be cooled down some. Who was he kidding?

Morning found the Murphys getting ready for church and not talking. The cold shoulder was something Joan did well. Murphy was used to it but that didn't make it any easier. His hope was that Mass would help ease the tension. After the Lord's Prayer when it was time to wish each other peace, that would break the silence, or so he hoped.

After Mass Joan started talking. "When are you going back to Saudi Arabia, Mike?"

"I don't know yet, Joan. I'm waiting to hear from Larry and you know how that goes. I should be here for another three weeks at least."

"I want the bathroom done before you leave. I'm sick and tired of using the bathroom downstairs."

To please her, he said, "Okay, That's fair."

Joan went on. "What about the yard?"

"If I can't get it raked off I will have someone take care of it."

Michael Murphy headed the car toward the shopping center and Joan picked up on it. "Where are we going now?"

"I have to pick up some jeans at the mall. You know it goes better when you help."

Joan had a better idea. "Why don't you go back to the house and work on the bathroom, and I will go to the mall. I don't need you with me to shop."

Murphy thought about it for a second and headed the car back to the house, "You got it, Joan."

Before Joan left the driveway Murphy made a list for her. After looking over the list, Joan seemed perplexed, saying, "Twelve pairs of 501 jeans? Why do you need twelve pairs of jeans? And why are there different sizes?"

Murphy looked at Joan and asked her to just please get what was on the list.

"These won't even fit you, they're too small," was her retort..

"Please Joan, just get what I put on the list, without second-guessing me."

But she went on, "Who are they for? They won't fit the Kellys either."

Murphy pressed on, "I'll explain the sizes later so please, Joan, just get what I asked for."

"This is all you need? You need twelve pairs of jeans that don't fit you?" Being a sharp woman, she simply wasn't going to let up.

"That's the list, no more, no less," he replied in a frustrated tone.

Murphy went to work on the bathroom project and Joan went to the mall for the jeans that were too small for her husband, although not happy about his evasive attitude. While Murphy was working on the bathroom he had a thought, I hope I don't have to eat alone again tonight.

KELLY'S CALL

Ten days had gone by and for the time being there had been peace in the valley. Murphy had worked steadily on the bathroom project and there clearly was progress. Joan did her day-to-day routine and was pleased but of course said nothing. Eventually an "attaboy" would come but Murphy had to keep his nose to the grindstone for that to happen.

That night the Murphys went out to dinner with some friends. Everything went well and a pleasant time was had by all. The drive home was quiet, and lucky for him there were no DWI checkpoints. Murphy was not driving poorly but that had no bearing on whether he could pass a breathalyzer test. Things had sure changed since he was a kid.

Michael and Joan had been asleep for about three hours when the phone started ringing. Murphy was awake instantly and had the phone in his hand. Glancing at the clock he recorded three o'clock across the face, 3:00 a.m.! He always tried to answer before Joan would wake up since that would surely mean trouble for him.

Murphy tried to whisper, "Hello," into the receiver. He heard nothing at first but static.

"Hello," he whispered the second time.

The next sound would answer the question which was, who the hell could this be?

The words came over the wire in a sort of slow motion.

"Y o u m o t h e r f u c k e r."

Murphy had heard this many times before, for at least thirty years. Larry Kelly loved to start a conversation in the middle of the night with these words.

"What do you want, Larry? Do you know what time it is, you asshole?"

"Oh sure, I'm an asshole. You don't write, you don't call, what am I, a piece of shit?"

"But it's three o'clock in the morning, Larry."

"Really, well, it's ten o'clock here," Larry replied.

"This couldn't wait until six o'clock your time, six in the evening?" Murphy was thinking that soon Joan would wake and be furious.

Kelly fired back, "I got you a job and this is how you talk to me. I suppose you're going to turn it down."

Murphy asked Kelly to hold for a minute while he changed phones. At that moment Joan rolled over and told Murphy to thank the jerk for waking her up. Murphy sighed, got up and asked his wife to hang up when he reached the downstairs phone. Upon reaching the downstairs phone Murphy picked it up and said, "OK." The receiver slammed down as he figured it would.

"I hope you're satisfied, Larry. Now I can have a miserable day with my wife. What's the deal anyway, Larry?"

"You know, Mike, I ask if you want a job and you give me some bullshit. We shoot the shit for a few minutes and then we hang up."

"Okay, just when would I have to start, Larry?"

There was a long pause and then Larry came back. "What did you say, Mike?"

"Are you deaf? I said, when would I start, Larry?"

Larry couldn't believe his ears. "Are you shitting me, Mike?"

"I'll say it again. Larry, when would I start?" Murphy couldn't believe he was asking this.

"Two weeks, man, two weeks. Then, you will do it! Don't say you will come if you're not serious, pal."

"I said it. I will be there. I'll FAX you a passport number in the morning. Is there anything else you need me to do?" Joan would be furious.

Kelly was elated. "No, that will do it. I can finish the rest of the paperwork; nothing has changed has it?"

"No, everything is the same as before."

I will have your paperwork processed through Houston. It won't take long, Mike. Now, what about Joan?"

"Oh, now you worry about Joan? I wish you would have thought about her a few minutes ago. But yeah, now the shit will hit the fan."

Larry couldn't hang up fast enough at this point. "I've got to go, talk to you in a few days." Just when Murphy was about to say, "Goodbye."

So now it was time to face Joan. Murphy decided to lie on the couch and face the music later...much later would have made him happy. Things were coming together sooner than he had planned. All Murphy could think of was how he could get the bathroom finished on time.

THE PROJECT

Ten days went by after the call and Murphy worked feverishly on the bathroom project. There was no talk of the upcoming job with Larry. What Joan never knew was how her husband grew nervous as the time to leave home approached. Leaving home used to be to support the family, so this time it was even harder. If Joan knew he was going back to the Kingdom to kidnap a child, and that's what it boiled down to, he might get his walking papers.

While at work in the bathroom Murphy heard their dog start to bark. Artie was small but when the mailman reached their front door all hell broke loose. He would run from the entrance to the TV room and back. Curtains would fly, rugs would fly and of course, Artie would fly. There was something about the mailman that the little guy just did not like. Joan and Mike often wondered about it but, try as they may, he could not be broken of the habit.

Murphy ran down the stairs to make sure the front door was closed properly; the last thing he wanted was for the dog to get out. As luck would have it, the door was in fact closed. All Artie could do was run back and forth. Murphy picked up the dog to calm him but even that took some time. Artie knew that once the mailman was done on their side he would come back down the other side of the street; that meant Act II.

As soon as the mailman was clear, Murphy opened the door and took the mail from the mailbox. This had to be done fast, for Artie was ready to go for at least thirty minutes. Looking through the usual stack of junk and letters, Murphy spotted an envelope from Houston. That didn't take long, he thought. Kelly must really need him in a bad way. Checking it out proved to be no surprise. Bottom line: British Air, 2200 hours,

Thursday night. Bounce at Heathrow and then on to Dhahran. He knew Kelly would be at the airport with coffee.

The project was a refinery with a connected pipeline and two pump stations. Murphy didn't give the description much thought. The usual shit was all that crossed his mind. Inspections for as long as he could stand it. One meeting after another and some day the almighty oil would flow.

Kelly was not to know the real reason for his accepting this project. He would play by the book until he could find the child. Please God that would not take too long, was his next thought. Now the time he hated was upon him: packing and leaving.

By the time Thursday came, Murphy had the bathroom done. He made arrangements to have the lawn done every week and the leaves raked when needed. Oil change for Joan's car was done and an inspection. Murphy knew that whatever he did would not be enough but it was always the same.

He packed at the last minute so that he would not have to have bags hanging around; that only made it harder. In an effort to carry only two bags, he went through the usual moves. He couldn't get fifteen pounds of shit in a ten-pound bag but he never stopped trying. Just when he thought he was done, Joan showed up with the twelve pairs of 501 jeans. Thank God, she didn't ask him once again who they were for. It was starting to look like two bags and one carryon. Out of the blue Joan came into the room with a pair of rosary beads. They belonged to his mother and he was grateful.

"I can't take those with me, Joan."

Joan looked puzzled. Suddenly it dawned on her and she left the room. When she returned she had another rosary; this pair was plastic and in rough shape.

"How about these, Mike?"

Mike smiled and thanked her. "You know how those airport guards are, sugar."

Joan handed Murphy a small box. It was about the size of a shoebox and he knew it contained goodies. She didn't know it, but he always choked inside when she did something like this. Just when the tension was getting high, she could make him feel so glad that she was his wife. He thought to himself that this was indeed the last time he would leave her like this.

When Thursday afternoon came, their goodbye was brief. Murphy took a train to New York City and then a bus to JFK airport. Once he was out of town things didn't hurt as much. The sooner he got to Dhahran, the sooner he would get back home.

THE FLIGHT

For some reason Michael Murphy always found the flight to England lonely and empty. People did have the chance to spread out over two or three seats once the flight was airborne. Most passengers didn't watch movies or listen to music with head phones. When it came time to have a snack, no interest was shown then either. This was a red eye at its best.

There were never any crying babies or loud passengers on this flight. Once the pilot introduced himself and the crew, there was no more mindless chatter for the rest of the trip. The attendants were strangers for the most part; if you needed one, they would answer your page. One could get a decent glass of wine on a British Air flight and that induced sleep. A window seat was no problem on this flight but there was never anything to see once you cleared the continental U.S. Murphy always looked for large ships but knew at thirty-five thousand feet, he was only kidding himself. The thought of putting on a life jacket in case of a ditch crossed his mind: where did she say it was and how do I inflate? He would always read the instructions in the back of the seat in front of him after that thought.

The arrival at Heathrow was about 7:00 a.m. No planes are supposed to land there during the night so this flight was one of the first of the day. Making his way to Customs was tiresome due to lack of a good rest. After Customs came the three-hour wait before departure to Dhahran. Murphy would hit the head to wash up and brush his teeth. With any luck he would not be interrupted by some Arab washing his feet in the basin next to him. At times like that, Murphy would finally give in to the fact that he was out of the country.

Once Murphy hit the shops and found something different to read, he still had two hours till boarding time. He would always think about having a drink…nothing like a Bloody Mary first thing in the morning. His second thought was the fact that there would be no more booze for him after they entered Saudi air space. The Brits used to get really pissed during the final leg of the flight. That's funny, he thought. He was already thinking in British terms: pissed is the British term for drunk.

The flight to Dhahran was not like the flight from New York. Now Murphy would be surrounded; there would not be an empty seat. There would be crying babies, loud Brits, Arab men who reeked of ladies' perfume, Western women who reeked of ladies' perfume and the smell of bug spray. Murphy never could get used to the way the attendants would spray some type of Raid throughout the plane before flight.

THE FLIGHT (2)

As luck would have it, Murphy was seated next to a chap from Ireland. While making small talk he found out that this was the Irishman's first trip to the Kingdom. John Walsh was going to be doing a job similar to Murphy's; Walsh was a welding inspector. He had taken a position with a company that Murphy was familiar with so they would probably see each other sooner or later.

Rather than enlighten Walsh about the local customs, Murphy thought it better that he found out for himself. He did let the harp know that he could call him any time, giving him Larry Kelly's number in case the need should arise. There was always a chance to get together for a meal, always nice to eat with someone from the West. Murphy figured Walsh would have his own opinion of the Kingdom formed by then.

Landing in Dhahran was always the end of freedom for Murphy. Sure you were not put in jail but you could not get out just because you may decide you had had enough. The airport was a nasty place and the first thing one noticed was the lack of women and children. Any kids that may have arrived on your flight just seemed to disappear with the ladies. Baggage was piled everywhere you looked. The baggage was in the form of cardboard boxes wrapped with many different color strings.

Passengers were dressed in turbans and robes. The absence of smiles on the passengers' waiting faces was evident. Strange smells were all around you, and to use the head you had to wade through some kind of wetness. The lights were out throughout the building; more were out than were on so you could not tell what you were wading through.

Lines were formed by the passengers waiting to board and passengers waiting to clear into the country. Walsh ended up in front of Murphy on the customs line. After about forty-five minutes they reached the customs officer. Walsh was instructed to empty his pockets and open his bags for inspection. Following instructions he placed his open bags on the table in front of the customs officer.

The first thing the little fellow did when he found a Playboy-type magazine was to peruse the magazine and smile. The next move made by the customs officer was to throw the magazine into the garbage pail. This brought a look of displeasure to Walsh's face. The customs officer looked straight into Walsh's eyes and laughed. This personal attack, as Murphy called it, went on for a full five minutes.

Finally the customs officer opened Walsh's shave kit. Removing each item from the kit, he examined them. When he came to Walsh's shaving brush he first looked at it and he then rubbed it all over his face with a big smile. Walsh moved forward as if to take the brush from the officer. Murphy grabbed Walsh's jacket from behind; Walsh stopped. Leaning forward, Murphy whispered into Walsh's ear: he wants you to do something stupid, John; be cool. Walsh stood still as the officer once again looked him in the eyes and laughed.

On the side of the shave kit was a zipper that was closed but the officer proceeded to open it. Sliding his fingers into the compartment he pulled out a card of some kind. The card as it turned out was from a wake that Walsh had attended years before. There was a picture of the Blessed Virgin Mary on one side and a prayer on the flip side for the deceased. After looking at the card for a minute or so the officer looked yet again into Walsh's eyes. "Marie" came from his lips with a Saudi accent and he smiled. Walsh, thinking that there was compassion there after all, smiled back. At that moment the customs officer came as close to getting the beating of his life as any man could come. Throwing the prayer card to the floor, he laughed out loud. Before Walsh could move, Murphy had him by the shoulder and again was holding him back. Be cool John, be cool.

The customs man looked at Walsh and smiled, "You have a problem?"

Walsh relaxed his body and to Murphy's surprise, smiled. "No, sir, I'm cool."

The customs man now directed Walsh through the line. Thank God that was over, Murphy thought. As Walsh cleared the line Murphy called to him, "Wait outside, John, and I will get you to your compound." Walsh gave Murphy a nod and proceeded out.

Murphy now emptied his pockets and presented his bags to the customs man. About fifteen minutes went by before Murphy cleared the line and joined the waiting Walsh. "You did great, John, I'm proud of you."

"If it were not for you, Michael, I think I would be in jail by now; thank you."

"No problem, partner." Reaching into his pocket Murphy pulled out a set of Rosary Beads and something else Walsh could not quite see.

"How the fuck did you get through with your beads, Michael?"

"They're plastic, John, so they don't show up on the metal detector. This ain't my first rodeo." Next Murphy handed Walsh his Mass Card.

"How did you do that?" As he took the card from Murphy's hand, a real smile came over his face.

"We have ways," Murphy replied, "we have ways."

MEETING KELLY

Dragging and carrying their bags Murphy and Walsh exited the airport entrance. The night air was hot and came over one like a tide. Murphy was always grateful that the nasty smells disappeared once you got outside the main terminal. The cabs resembled a used car lot owned by someone you would never buy from. Dents, cracked windshields, antennas made of metal coat hangers, and bent bumpers comprised the fleet. The drivers…well, that was another story.

Michael Murphy digressed for a moment and then caught himself: Kelly. No sooner had the thought of Larry Kelly crossed his mind than he felt a hand on his shoulder. Turning quickly to his right side he heard and saw Larry Kelly.

"Cab, sir?" Murphy had to believe Kelly knew how relieved they were to see him.

A smile came over the faces of both men followed by a hand shake and a brotherly hug. Murphy turned to John Walsh while still shaking Kelly's hand. "Larry, I want you to meet John Walsh, another harp in the Kingdom."

Kelly smiled and extended his hand to Walsh. "Welcome aboard, John."

"Can we give John a lift to his compound, Larry?" Murphy offered.

"No problem. I have my pickup across the street and it's empty. Seating might be tight but I'm sure we can make it. What compound are you being housed at, John?"

"I think it's referred to as Al Zarod, Larry."

"Okay, that's on our way; you're in luck. Mike won't have to sit on your lap for too long."

Murphy jeered at Kelly. "I can sit in the back, asshole."

"Easy partner, I'm only kidding," responded Larry.

Obviously relieved, John remarked, "I really appreciate this, Larry; the cab system looks a bit sketchy."

Larry smiled at Walsh and winked, referring to Murphy, "You should have seen this clown the first time he landed here." The three men assembled the baggage and headed out for the parking lot.

Larry asked, "Who are you here for, John?"

"Shaker, Larry."

"Did they tell you what project you would be on?"

"Yup, I'm to test welds here in town; they have a shop near the compound."

"And what kind of hours are you working?"

Murphy turned to Kelly. "You're writing a book, Larry?"

"This is how you treat me after I get up in the middle of the night to pick you up? What am I, just a piece of shit?" Larry acted indignant.

But Mike, thinking that Larry was going on too much, said, "Hold the third degree until he gets his feet wet, for God's sake."

Walsh looked a bit uncomfortable. "I don't mean to start a problem."

"This is normal, John. Larry has to know everything about everybody. Just tell him to fuck off."

Suddenly Walsh realized he was dealing with two men who were indeed good friends. He felt that meeting Murphy and Kelly was a real stroke of luck.

Within an hour John Walsh was at his new home away from home. The compound looked fine.... a nice-sized pool, tennis courts, and an exercise area with bicycles available. Now if he should find a nice dining hall for breakfast he would have it made. Murphy and Kelly wished Walsh the best of luck and gave him their numbers to call once the dust had settled. Walsh thanked his two new friends once again and entered the lobby; he was very tired.

WELCOME BACK

Larry and Michael Murphy drove on to the Resiot Compound in Dhahran. Compound for compound, the Resiot was still one of the best in Dhahran. Most of the newer compounds had been modeled after her since she was one of the original done in the Sixties. Entering the main gate Murphy strained to remember how many men he had known in this compound. He knew some were still here, like Larry, some must have moved on, and he knew some were dead. Worst of all, he thought, he was back.

"How long have you been living here, Larry?" Michael began.

"Fourteen years off and on. Why do you ask, Michael?"

Reflecting on the length of time he'd been away from the States, Michael replied, "Wow, it's time you got back home, Larry. This is no way to spend your sixties, pal."

"One more year for me, Michael."

"But, you told me that five years ago, Larry."

Larry looked at Michael and smiled, "You came back; y'know, you told me the exact same thing four years ago."

"Yeah, I did," Murphy confessed, "I did."

Larry thought for a minute before saying, "So, what's Joan think about your coming back?"

"What do you think?"

"Then, why did you come back?" Larry was thinking if the situation was that bad, why do it?

"Top secret mission, Larry; if I tell you I will have to kill you," as the expression went.

"Right; I understand!" Larry chuckled, as he continued, "Did Joan ever get her legs fixed?"

"Larry, you really need to get some sleep," as he was searching his brain to remember the details of that long-ago circumstance.

"Really, come on, Mike, remember how they were all black?" Larry prodded.

Larry was referring to an incident that Murphy had experienced while working in Yambu, on the Red Sea. He had received a nice fat letter from home. Upon opening it he found a number of pictures of Joan and their kids on a beach in Connecticut. Their daughters were ten and seven at the time and it looked as if the weather was beautiful. As Mike checked out each picture he became happy and sad at the same time; he hated being away from them, but at least they had good days.

The girls frolicked in the surf, their smiles infectious. Picture after picture passed in front of Murphy and then something strange happened. For some reason a picture appeared that was wrong, something was wrong. The shot was of Joan standing with the surf behind her. Joan was wearing a two piece bathing suit and...then it hit him: her legs where painted black. Murphy could not believe what he was seeing. Someone had gone through his mail and at the sight of his wife's bare legs, they saw fit to paint them black.

For weeks he had found that his mail was always in rough shape by the time it got to him; however, this was too much. The religious police had gone through his mail and he was looking at the result. Murphy was furious but he knew there was nothing he could do about it.

Murphy received a call from Joan and the kids each Sunday at three o'clock at his office. When Joan called that Sunday he told her what had happened. By then he had calmed down and had a plan. I'm going to bring the picture back with me, he explained to Joan. Have another shot made for me so we can show the folks back home both the U.S. and the Middle East versions. I want the kids to see what goes on in other countries; perhaps they will appreciate the freedom they have a little bit more.

Coming back to the present, Murphy went on, "We got her legs fixed, Larry, they're all white again." He simply wanted to put that experience in the past. "Larry, I need to get some sleep. Let's talk business later; it's been a long day. Give me a call in six or seven hours, or you could actually make it eight."

"You got it, brother," Larry replied. "Welcome back."

THE COMPANY

Michael Murphy woke to someone beating on his door. He knew it could be only one person with that type of an approach unless it was the police: Kelly.

"I'm coming, Larry, stop beating on the door, will you."

Getting out of bed was really hard although by the clock he could see he had gotten seven hours sleep. Murphy reached for the door and found that turning the door knob was a task. As he pulled the door open, the sight that was to appear stopped him in his tracks. There was Kelly, pants down to his ankles, bent over with his large ass facing into his room and his cheeks spread.
"Good morning, Michael."

All Murphy could do was say good morning back. Larry was famous for mooning and he had forgotten.

After getting his pants back up and turning around, Larry extended his hand to shake.

"I don't think so, brother."

"What? My hands are clean."

"What about that thing you just had them wrapped around?"

"It's clean, too."

"When are you going to start wearing undershorts, Larry?"

"I don't need them, I wipe myself. And I have a great hose in my room."

"Spare me, Larry. Come on in."

"Did you get enough sleep, Mike?"

"You know the routine, Larry. It won't hurt until tomorrow. Two or three days from now I'll be fine."

"Get ready and we can have lunch. I want to run you over to the office and get you a truck."

"Give me a half hour, Larry. I'll meet you at the dining hall."

"OK. Oh, and I got you some walking around money, Michael."

"Thanks, Larry."

THE COMPANY, PART TWO

Murphy got his heart beating and made it to the dining hall in forty minutes flat. After checking in with the man at the door, he proceeded into the large room. The fellow at the door was different but had the same routine. He sat behind a desk that had nothing on it but a clipboard and a newspaper. Murphy figured the chap was from India based on his looks. His accent gave the same impression and there was something about the way he wagged his head.

Years earlier Murphy found out that men from the Near East didn't nod yes or no; the motion was somewhere in between which resembled a bobble-head doll. The only time it got on his nerves was on the job when men would say yes and nod no, or say no and nod yes.

His black suit was well worn with a tie that had not missed a day in months. His shirt on the other hand could be white, yellow, blue, or black which Murphy called the Johnny Cash look. Hair was jet black and stacked high and wavy. In his country he would probably be found quite a handsome chap. Murphy could only see a fellow who should be dancing with a girl in a Hollywood production.

Reaching the food line brought back even more memories and they were not good. Many times the food did not look like what the menu said was being served. Murphy found himself reaching for bread and proceeding straight to the soup. Damn, he thought, apple orange soup, where do they come up with this stuff? So a bowl of apple orange soup and lots of bread would have to do it. All one has to add to this is a half a bottle of Tabasco sauce and you have it: hot sauce soup. Leaving the line with his gourmet meal, Murphy began looking for Kelly. Nothing changes; Kelly was sitting right next to the coffee pot. Kelly probably drank ten cups of coffee a day.

"So, do you feel better, Michael?"

Joining Kelly, Murphy replied, "Yes," then began moving his head in the bobble-head doll fashion of the locale..

It was then that Kelly, in his hearty guffaw manner familiar to me, added, "You're going to fit right in, Murphy."

"Okay, so what's on the agenda, Larry?"

"I'm afraid more than I can handle. I have six projects I need you to watch. Two are office complex-type projects, three are housing projects, and then I have a Mosque."

In a surprised tone, Michael inquired, a Mosque?"

"Believe it or not, that's right, a Mosque," came his reply.

"That's incredible! They're going to let an infidel into a Mosque?" he stammered.

"And you're safe until the end of construction," Larry remarked.

"Okay, Larry, whatever you say." Michael went on, "But who is doing the offices?"

Larry explained, "Most of the guys are from the Philippines; you may remember some of them. I told them you were the inspector and a couple of them remembered you. I'm not sure who got the houses but you won't have any problems with them once they know your act. There is one more thing, Mike, we only have six months to get this done."

This was like music to the old man's ears. If he couldn't get the job done in that time (the real job), he would have to leave anyway. Plenty of time to make a plan, plenty of time, he hoped, to find little Marie. Murphy's meal didn't take long to eat and by then Larry had just finished his fourth cup of coffee.

"Meet me outside, Mike, I have to take a shit. The truck is open and the keys are in it. Don't fuck with the radio," uttered Larry in his very familiar gruff manner.

Laughing, Murphy gave Kelly some more bobble head. "Yes, Mr. Larry Sir."

"Thought you would like to know that Peter and Paul are all excited about your coming back to work with us, Mike," Larry said on his way outside.

Michael was amazed. "They're still here after all this time?"

Larry thinking it strange, said, "Why should they go home, Mike?"

At that, Murphy and Kelly left the room and went their separate ways.

CHECKING IN

The drive to Ademco's office brought back more memories for Michael Murphy. Now that it was daylight he could see that not much had changed in Dhahran. Between some buildings there still appeared to be large lots that resembled desert. Plastic bags lined the highways and fences along same. Red lights were something you were supposed to stop at, if you wanted to. Should you choose to continue through a red light, you merely flashed your headlights as you approached.

Now and then one would see a large tent near the road with a Maserati parked next to it; he always got a kick out of that. Beat up old pickup trucks carted camels around which were hobbled and had legs folded under them. Every other car you saw was a Chevy Caprice with some still having a Jesus Fish on the bumper. It was not hard to figure out which cars had been brought in from Stateside. Seeing a Muslim driving a Caprice with a fish on the bumper was another thing that brought a smile to Murphy's face. Arabs with new cars were easy to spot in the Kingdom also; they never remove the window stickers that describe the options and cost of the vehicle.

Kelly glanced over at Murphy and asked him if it felt good to be back.

"Can't remember the last time I felt this good, Larry; maybe I never have."

"Why do you always have to be so negative, brother?" Larry continued. "How come you came back, Michael?"

Murphy knew that Larry was no fool so he just said, "Money; why do you stay here, Larry?"

"Oh, not so fast, Michael. You gave in too easily. It's gotten to be a game with us; I call and tell you I need you and you just say, 'no, thank you.' So what's really going on here?"

Michael was hedging. "Larry, I can tell you that this is the last time. What I save on this trip will finance my next passage which will be across the Atlantic.

"And that's OK with Joan?" a surprised Larry blurted out.

"What do you think?"

Knowing his friend well, Larry just glanced at Murphy and smiled, "You really are crazy, Michael."

Murphy said, "Tell me something I don't already know, Larry."

Kelly wheeled his pickup into the Ademco parking lot. Pickup trucks lined the front of the building while small cars lined both sides. The complex was in fact a number of job trailers tied together to form a square with a garden in the center and park benches. The lobby was simple, i.e., one desk with chairs for those who had to wait to be seen. A Philippine secretary sat at the desk, male of course. There were no pictures on the walls but there were awards from clients who they had done projects for. Larry proceeded past the secretary and gave the little fellow a nod. The secretary in turn nodded and wished "Mr. Larry" a good afternoon.

As the two men entered the inner office Larry Kelly shouted out, "What, no coffee? What am I, a piece of shit?" At those remarks, two more Filipinos jumped to their feet and darted toward the coffee mess. "One minute, Mr. Larry; it will be ready in one minute." Both men prepared the coffee pot which was done in a matter of seconds. They turned back to Kelly and both had big smiles for him.

"We were not sure when you were going to be here, Mr. Larry." As both men spotted Michael Murphy at the same time, they greeted him with, "Mr. Michael, how are you?" They raced to his side with outstretched hands and larger-than-life smiles. "So good to see you once again, Mr. Michael, so good to see you." Murphy shook hands with the two men and, of course, returned the smiles. It was good to see Peter and Paul after all these years. They had not changed much: both very slight, both like little children. Neither one of them could have weighed more than one hundred pounds, both about five-foot-two, both had white shirts, blue ties, blue slacks, and black loafers.

Murphy patted both men on their shoulders and told them how glad he was to see them again. "You guys haven't changed a bit. How is it that I got old and you guys are still the same?"

Peter and Paul laughed and thanked Murphy for his kind words and then expressed, "Mr. Larry was so happy when you consented to return, Mr. Michael."

As Kelly reached for the coffee pot he turned to Peter and Paul, cautioning, "Don't tell him that."

They laughed and went on. "The truth is that he needed someone he could send out and not have to hold their hand."

Kelly again told the two men to stop talking, warning, "Murphy's head is big enough already."

"We shall need your passport, Mr. Michael. We have a pickup ready for you, number 215."

Murphy was happy to get that number on his truck, thinking 215 was one of his lucky numbers.

They continued, "By tomorrow we should have your Egamma ready," meaning an Arab passport. You cannot leave the country with it but only travel about the Kingdom. This was something Murphy never liked: he hated giving up his U.S. Passport.

"Your license will be ready tomorrow, too, but you will need another blood test. We can arrange for that first thing in the morning if you like."

"Go for it," Murphy replied.

The last blood test was something he never forgot. A Filipino nurse inserted a needle into his vain. One tube from the needle went into a bottle about the size of a shot glass and another tube left the bottle cap. This second one the nurse would suck on and when the bottled was filled, the sucking would stop. Hmmm. technology at its best, he used to think.

Larry accompanied Michael. "Do you have some paperwork for me on the projects and their locations, Larry?"

"It will be here for you in the morning. You can spend the day going over the prints and getting over your jet lag. I'm leaving town for a few days but you have my number."

Murphy thanked Peter and Paul for their help and took the keys to his pickup. Bidding Kelly a fond farewell, saying, "I need more sleep guys so I shall see you in the morning," Michael departed.

The good part was that Kelly was leaving town for a few days, Murphy thought. He needed to speak to Peter and Paul alone as soon as possible. Things were coming together better than he could have hoped but for now sleep was all he wanted.

THE ASSIGNMENTS

By the afternoon of the following day Murphy finally loaded his still-tired body into the company pickup. Clearing the compound he noticed that there was no guard on the gate and the gate was, in fact, wide open. This was not a normal occurrence and Murphy made a mental note to find out what was going on with security. The weather was as usual, warm and sunny, and the sky was always a deep blue without a cloud in sight. Murphy thought to himself how good it was to be an Arab… you never had to wonder what to wear or what the weather would be like today. Men wear white and women wear black. On the other hand, he thought, I like the four seasons.

Entering the parking lot it looked as if nothing had moved since yesterday: pickups in front, cars on both sides. Murphy parked his truck in the same spot where he had removed it the day before.

Murphy walked past the little fellow at the front desk and greeted him with, "A good afternoon, partner." The little fellow jumped to his feet and replied, "Good afternoon, Mr. Michael, Peter and Paul have been expecting you, sir." It was at that moment that Murphy remembered the blood test, the one he had forgotten to go to that morning.

The main office area was quiet except for Peter and Paul who sat at their respective desks.

Startling them somewhat, Murphy spoke, "Gentleman, good afternoon."

Both men sprang up and raced to Murphy's side with hands extended, "Hello, Mr. Michael," came the chorus.

One thing about their manners, Murphy thought, is they always make you feel like they are glad to see you. In the States very often people treat you as if you're an interruption. "The bad news is that I forgot my blood test, guys, I'm sorry."

"No problem, Mr. Michael, we can take care of that on Sunday."

Murphy also forgot that Friday and Saturday was the weekend in the Middle East. He was thinking he had to be retrained again.

Peter picked up a package from his desk and, handing it to Murphy, said, "Your Egamma is ready, Mr. Michael." It looked similar to a passport. Going on he said, "Also in the package, Mr. Michael, is your license and on Monday your blood type can be stapled to that."

Murphy took the package and slid it into his jacket pocket. "Peter, I have a question for you; have you got a few minutes?"

"Oh, yes, Sir, Mr. Michael. What can we do for you?"

"You see, I would like to contact a friend of mine and surprise him now that I'm back. I checked the phone book but his name is nowhere to be found."

"Well, what is his name, Mr. Michael?"

"Fozi... Al Fozie."

Both Peter and Paul reached for phone books at the same time. After a few seconds went by each of them came up with the same reaction: no one listed by that name.

"Peter, I think he is working for one of the oil companies here in Dhahran. How many oil companies are there in Dhahran now?"

Paul piped up with, "Five, maybe six. Who did he work for when you were here last?"

"Well, that's the problem, Paul; he didn't work for an oil company in those days. I figured you guys could check with your connections; I know that if you can't find him he would have to be dead."

"Oh, Mr. Michael, we will give it a try but things aren't the way they used to be. Some companies don't hire people from the Philippines anymore."

Murphy acted surprised, "What? How do they expect to keep any order in these offices, Peter?"

"Thank you, Mr. Michael, you are very kind. We wish they saw things the way you do. Paul and I will give it a try but we can't promise anything."

"Fine, I can't ask for more than that, my friend. Let me know if it works out. If it's not in the cards, oh, well."

"We can promise you that if something comes up we will let Mr. Larry know."

Murphy got a funny feeling suddenly. With any luck the guys had not picked up on it. He went on, "I want to surprise Fozi and I want to surprise Larry; he knows Fozi too. Can we keep it just between us so I can have some fun with them?"

"Of course, Mr. Michael, we got it; our lips are sealed."

"You guys are the best. I won't forget my blood test Monday and again, I am sorry for missing it."

"Oh, it's simply jet lag, Mr. Michael." Peter and Paul stood there smiling from ear to ear thinking they were in on a big surprise.

"Now, what about my assignments? You have some prints for me?" Michael nonchalantly changed the subject.

"Yes, sir, the housing is one package, the office complexes are another package, and the Mosque is very light. No one would take the Mosque, Mr. Michael; Mr. Larry was afraid he would have to do it himself."

"Very interesting," Murphy replied. "Can I use one of your print tables, Peter?

"Certainly, sir. There are two open in C wing. Would you like some coffee or tea, sir?" they continued, trying to please Michael.

"No, thank you; this time of the day that would make me pee every half hour." Murphy was already feeling the urge from the day's volume.

Peter and Paul both laughed when they heard that. Murphy thought to himself: these guys must be the happiest guys in the Kingdom, always laughing.

For the next two hours Murphy would go over the prints. No special items that he could see; the usual shit. The Mosque was very simple and he found himself treating it in a respectful manner. Not good to mess with religion, anybody's religion, he reflected.

Ahead of Murphy was a two-day break... the weekend. In the old days he would be racing on the Gulf at Sunset Cove. Since the cove may be included in his version of the great escape, he planned to visit it tomorrow. He wondered if there were still a lot of sailboats on anchor in the cove. It used to amaze Murphy how many sailboats were on anchor and never moved. Perhaps he would have to use one for a short sail to Bahrain. Murphy wondered if any of the old crew would still be at the cove tomorrow, a hangout for Westerners on the weekend. The Arabs used to motor just off shore in hopes of seeing Western women in bathing suits. The Brits used to get pissed and shake their fists at them.

SUNSET COVE YACHT CLUB

Friday morning found Murphy in a better state of mind; he had probably slept for twelve hours. After breakfast he fired up his pickup and headed for Sunset Cove. Sailboat racing had always been a release for Michael Murphy and no matter where he worked, there always seemed to be a body of water. Puget Sound in Washington, Long Island Sound in Connecticut., the Red Sea while inspecting from the Jeddah office of the Kingdom, the Hudson River in New York, and the Persian Gulf here in Dhahran.

Four years ago he had teamed up with a fellow from India; together they got a second for the season in their class and second overall for all classes. Zarir Blon held an American passport but was born in India. They had been introduced by a fellow inspector named Dick Smith who knew Zarir needed crew who was experienced. Together they would dominate the Hobie 17 class whenever Dick Smith was not around; Dick was the best.

Dick was an Aussie who had been raised on the water. At five-foot-eight and one hundred and fifty pounds, Dick could sail with or without a crew and win every time. The Smiths had three children who would climb onto their catamaran, the oldest being their ten-year-old daughter, and set records. Some of the fleet racers would protest that Dick had too many people on his boat but their combined weight was a little over one hundred pounds.

Dick's wife, Mary, was from Canada. They met while Dick was in college in Vancouver, BC. Mary spent her time making quilts, acting as an aide at the school, keeping house at their compound, and watching their two little boys. The Smiths had been married for fifteen years and lived in the Kingdom for the past eleven years. Murphy and the Smiths had grown very close and Murphy used to babysit the kids on occasion.

Zarir was a tall man with thick black hair. He weighed in at about two-hundred-and-twenty pounds and stood about six-two. He was relatively new at sailing and therefore not aware of the rules of the road. Murphy had spent hours reading books on racing rules and techniques and was not afraid to take a chance. In a short time Murphy taught Zarir how to screw someone by the book, the way gentlemen do it. Zarir was in his fifties and very laid back. And, when sailing, Murphy didn't mind confrontation so together they made one hell of a team.

Once you leave Dhahran proper you are in the desert. The roads are still four lane and there is a median. When driving to Sunset Cove the last thing one sees is the world's biggest flea market. You can buy most anything for the home or tent, you can ride a camel, you can purchase a parakeet in any color you want. If you don't see one that is the correct color, they will gladly spray paint one for you. It took some time but Murphy figured out how the different colors came about, any parakeet, any color, sort of like Earl Scheib. There were kiddy rides for the children and camel races where you could participate in if you were crazy.

Eventually there would be desert on one side and shore line on the other. The water was blue and the sand was nearly pure white. The contrast was magnificent and seldom did you see people, not at all like the beaches at home, Murphy thought. Now and then you might spot a tent or some cars but not very often.

Out of nowhere Murphy spotted about ten women all running in the same direction; they were covered in black and he was not sure if something was wrong. On second glance Murphy saw what was causing the women to all run along the beach in the same direction: they were chasing a soccer ball. He then spotted a few more women in the water and, of course, they were covered all in black. 100 degrees F. was not uncommon for that time of the morning and that had to be a tough color to have on.

Murphy finally made it to the Sunset Cove turn off. Nothing looked different, even the guards looked the same. Pulling up to the guard shack Murphy flashed his Egamma and stopped. One of the guards walked around his pickup looking at nothing in particular. Next came the wave through as the gate raised. The drive to the beach and launching area took another five minutes and this also had not changed.

Arriving early gave Murphy a chance to check out the sailboat fleet on the moorings. The mooring fleet was located about two hundred feet from shore and he counted something like thirty yachts. He knew he would have to find a way to row out and inspect each craft.

Waterline marks tell a lot about a yacht: how long they have been in the water, how much water may be in the boat, how often they are used, and then one could check to see how the cabins were secured. The standing rigging was important also. Was it loose? Was it too tight? One thing you don't need is to have your mast fall; Bahrain was too far to swim to. From shore Murphy could not tell which yachts may have had inboard motors and then there was the question of which had sails aboard. Some skippers remove their sails when the yacht will not be used regularly.

Suddenly Murphy thought of what was at stake here. For some reason he had not given the escape plan that much thought, until now. He needed a vehicle he could trust, he needed bad weather, he would have no crew, and then there was the child. The child…that was another story.

>From behind Murphy came the sound of a vehicle in the parking lot. If nothing else it pulled him out of the trance he was entering. All he could hope for at this point was someone he might know to show up. One thing he could do was to ask around and obtain a crew position; someone always needed crew.

OLD FRIENDS

Murphy dropped the tailgate on his pickup and took a seat. Pulling his duffel bag to him he opened the zipper, all three feet of it. He knew people would continue to arrive for the next hour and he would use this time to get his gear ready.

The first thing he pulled out was a water shoe, the left side. Reaching back into the bag his hand fished around until he felt the shoe for the right side, placing it next to the left shoe. He thought to himself, good deal, a pair. Next he would fish for his knee pads, good deal, a pair. Stop watch, how long has it been since he saw that thing? Digging around proved fruitless, no stop watch. Perhaps he would find the watch in one of the small zipper compartments. Sailing gloves: these seemed to fall into his right hand.

I should try looking in the bag, he thought; no, that would be too easy and he couldn't see the cars that were entering the parking lot. Sun block, again he fished, again his hand recognized the feel and it was on the tailgate. Cheap sun glasses, can't lose another pair of Raybans. Over the course of twenty-eight years Murphy had lost a dozen pair of Raybans…rivers, creeks, streams, oceans, and bays all had them now. Unzipping the compartment on one end of the duffel bag, Murphy was happy to find not only his cheap sun glasses but, lo and behold, the stop watch was in there, too. In the end he figured he had more shit hanging off him than a Thanksgiving turkey had.

"Is that you, Michael?"

Murphy turned to see a smiling Mary Smith walking toward him.

"Holy, it is you!"

Returning her smile which stretched from ear to ear, Murphy stood up and walked toward Mary. "It really is me, kid," he was happy to report.

They hugged and Murphy lifted Mary off the ground. "Put me down, Michael Murphy. Where have you been and why didn't you keep in touch?" At that, Mary turned and looked back up the parking lot, yelling, "Dick, we've got our babysitter back."

Murphy looked in the same direction and there he was, Dick Smith. This was more than he could hope for. Dick and Mary were truly a sight for sore eyes. Michael and Dick hugged and then Mary joined in. There is nothing like old friends, nothing in this world. The three people hugged and laughed for what seemed like a long time. "How the hell are you, Michael?" Dick inquired. "When did you get back? Where are you staying? Where have you been?"

Murphy was as excited to see them as vice versa. "Hold on, Dick, one question at a time." He then explained everything to them and they all ended up on the tailgate. "How are the kids? Where are the kids?" came the questions tumbling out of Michael's mouth.

"They won't be here today, Michael, but they still ask about you."

"Wow, they remember me after all this time?" Murphy went on to say.

In unison, the Smiths chimed "You bet; they call you the guy who used to juggle for them. Okay, now down to business. Are you looking for a crew position?"

"Sure, yes I am, Dick. Is Zarir still here?"

"No, he retired two months ago; good for him but not for us. He moved back to the States and planned to contact you once he got settled."

"Hmm, I haven't heard anything from him yet."

"Oh, but you will for sure," Mary said.

"Well that settles it, you have to crew for me today, Michael," Dick happily responded.

Murphy jumped at the opportunity, "I would love to, Dick."

There was time before the start of the race. So Dick declared, "We have three hours till the gun, how about some breakfast?"

"I could sure use some coffee. Is it still nasty swill?"

Grimacing, Dick countered, "Sorry to say, the same awful stuff, Michael."

Over coffee Murphy and the Smiths rehashed old times: races, babysitting, sneaking into church, and wine making. Those where the days! Murphy moved his shoulders in such a way that it appeared they were sore.

Mary picked up on the motion right away. "What's the matter with your shoulders, Michael?"

"It's just that I'm a bit stiff, kid. Maybe I need something to relax my shoulders," Michael continued as he shifted and stretched so more.

"Are you asking for a back rub?" Mary said, showing concern.

Looking around the yard, Murphy suggested, "I feel as if I would like to row. Do you think there are there any dinks available?"

At that, Dick pointed toward the north point. "My inflatable is right over there. It'd only take a few minutes to blow it up. I usually put our five-horse on it but you can row it if you like."

"You sure you don't mind if I take it out, Dick?"

"Not at all, Michael. You're always welcome to use it. You can row for an hour if you want to, we have plenty of time."

The two men began to set up the inflatable and within a half hour or so, they pushed it into the water. Murphy climbed into the craft and took the oars in hand. It didn't take long to get a rhythm going and Murphy was headed out to the mooring field. It definitely felt good to be on the water…he always liked rowing.

THE GETAWAY BOAT SEARCH

Rowing toward the mooring field Murphy first changed direction and went into a large circle. As the circles got larger he finally ended up passing through the mooring field. There were five rows of yachts with about six yachts per row. He continued circling until he was in the farthest row. At no time did he look directly at any yacht. As he finally passed the sixth row he slowed down and simulated bends at the hip as if he were trying to touch his toes. With the rowing motion stopped, Murphy drifted slowly to a stop toward the outside center of the last row.

Two of the boats appeared to be low in the water, not good. One was actually high in the water which made him think there were no sails, no motor, probably no water in the holding tanks, and maybe no electronics. The last three looked promising although he could not see if they had locks on the companionway entrances. Murphy now stood up in the inflatable as if to stretch, giving him a chance to look into each of the last three yachts as he drifted slowly past. The largest of these three was in fact, open; the other two had locks of some kind.

In sailboat lingo, the larger or longer the boat, the faster the boat. Murphy made a mental note that there was only one yacht in the last row out that he could consider. Taking a seat he began rowing once again, another circle that would take him into the next row. Out of the next six he found only one yacht that might do but it had a lock on the companionway entrance, again making a mental note. Moving in between the next two rows proved fruitless, all small and all locked. So that was it, two yachts out of eighteen and one of them was locked up. As for the three remaining rows, he just rowed through and paid no attention. A yacht missing from any of the first three rows would stick out like a sore thumb.

Murphy started back toward the shoreline to join Dick Smith. There were now about fifteen catamarans lined up on shore and soon it would be off to the races. After putting the inflatable away Murphy headed over to the skippers meeting to meet Dick Smith.

"Feeling any better, Michael, after your excursion?" Smith asked, seeing Murphy return.

"You bet I do and now I'm ready to race. "

"I saw you standing up out there, Michael, thought I might have to rescue you." Dick was thinking that maybe Murphy hadn't gotten his sea legs back.

"I still have some ability left as far as balance, Dick. I'm not that rusty or old, yet."

"Well, I'm counting on you, Michael. We have ten to fifteen knots of wind already and it's expected to pick up even more." Smith was contemplating the stiff breezes with a boat wanting to heel, and that he would need a "gorilla" today, for sure.

Those remarks only made Murphy happier. "Bring it on, partner; the stronger the wind, the more exhilarating for me. You know that."

"That's music to my ears!" Dick went on.

Murphy excused himself and walked over to his pickup. Taking a notebook out of his duffel bag he drew the last three rows of yachts and circled the possibles. Now would come the hard part: breaking and entering. Perhaps tomorrow morning he could arrive early and row some more after arranging that with Dick. For now it was props, costumes, and show time.

By the end of the day, as Yogi always says, "It's déjà vu all over again." Dick Smith sailed a flawless race as usual. They were so far out front that by the time the second catamaran finished, they were all put away and drinking tea with Mary.

THE SEARCH, DAY TWO

Friday morning found Michael Murphy up early once again and Sunset Cove bound. He gave himself an extra hour to exercise or row before the club members began to arrive for the races. The guards did their inspection once again of nothing in particular at the main gate. Finding no problems Murphy was waved through as the gate opened. Since this would be his last visit to the cove until next weekend, Murphy avoided small talk with the guards. "Thank you, gentlemen" was all he said.

Proceeding on to the beach and parking lot Murphy noticed that the windsock was standing straight out which indicated that the wind was from the south. There had to be fifteen knots of wind already and it was still early. Sailing today would be fun but rowing would be a handful.

After getting the inflatable ready and over to the water's edge, Murphy shoved off. There was no reason to pretend that this was all about exercise today. Being this early he rowed directly out to the mooring field. Due to the high winds all the yachts were facing due south. As he had figured the inflatable wanted to do nothing but head north. He worked very hard to bring the little craft to the south side of the mooring field past the outside row. Once there he could drift by each yacht for his second inspection. The fourth yacht, the one that was not locked up, was still the only prospect.

Since the wind took him past the whole row quickly he turned the inflatable into the wind once again and headed for the beginning of the row. This is too much like work, Murphy thought but it had to be done. As he began drifting back down the outside row he checked the shore for any signs of life. Seeing no problems he brought the inflatable alongside the open yacht. Grabbing a cleat near the transom, Murphy tied off and let the inflatable settle in behind the yacht. Once again he checked the shoreline where he saw no cars or trucks parked.

Climbing over the port side of the yacht while staying as low as possible, Murphy lowered himself into the cockpit. Another check of the shore line showed clean and green, time to go below. Sliding the three hatch boards out one at a time went well: sometimes hatch boards stick from swelling due to salt water. Another peek toward shore showed no problems.

Sliding into the cabin head first, Murphy lost his grip, landing on his head and right shoulder while the rest of his body flipped over him. Lying flat out on the cabin sole, Murphy felt for something he could pull himself up with. A rail around the settee served the purpose. He hoped he had not bruised his face; he wasn't looking forward to any explaining of that.

This is good, he thought, as his head didn't hit the cabin top when standing straight up. Two large bunks/settees comprised the main salon. Looking back toward the stern and companionway entrance he saw the galley, the one he had tumbled past during his fall. Looking forward he saw a door that was closed, opening it to find a head on the port (left) side and a storage compartment to starboard. Beyond that was a V berth that would hold two comfortably.

This has to be somewhere between 28 and 30 feet long, Murphy decided; perfect. Looking out through a porthole on the starboard side Murphy still saw no action on the beach or parking lot. The V berth was full of sail bags and life jackets. The galley cabinets were empty, no canned food or water. After finding the water holding tanks, an inspection showed them to be half full. Murphy removed the stairs under the companionway, the ones he had fallen down. This was his first sign of a problem, no motor! The motor had been removed and the space was being used for storage. My kind of a sailor, Murphy thought; after all, they call them sailboats, don't they?

Another check of the shore and Murphy climbed out of the cabin. Next week I will check the other prospect and see if that yacht has had any sign of usage. Installing the hatch boards Murphy slid the hatch cover back over them. Two instruments were located either side of the companionway, a compass on the port side and a knot meter on the left side. It dawned on him that he had seen no battery below which spelled another problem. Need a battery for instrument lights, he thought, have to check on that next time I drop in. As the thought went through his mind he rubbed his head.

Sliding over the side of the yacht and into the inflatable went better than his descent into the cabin. Untying the line, Murphy pushed off and the wind did the rest. Drifting down the line he began rowing for shore as soon as he cleared the last yacht. As luck would have it the first car pulled into the parking lot as Murphy reached shore.

The rest of the day was a repeat of the day before. Smith and his crew, Michael Murphy, won the race. He ate a late lunch with the Smith family and became homesick. While there were no bruises visible on his face, he did have one hell of a lump on his gourd. Murphy said his goodbyes and headed out for his compound and some sorely-need aspirin. With any luck he had found the getaway boat. Next week would tell the story.

BACK TO WORK

Saturday morning found Murphy up and finished with breakfast by seven o'clock. The drive to the office went well since not many Arabs are out at that time of day, kind of like back home. There were a few open spots in the parking lot as Murphy observed that most of the inspectors, like him, were early birds. After parking he made his way through the lobby and inner office area without having to return one greeting. Returning to C wing Murphy found that only one print table was available; four more inspectors were present this morning.

Looking about the room Murphy piped up with, "Good morning, gents."

Two of the inspectors returned his greeting, one grunted, and the fourth one said nothing.

Murphy walked over to the two who had returned his good morning and introduced himself. The first man was Pat MacFarland, a plumbing inspector. The second man was Ralph Davenport; his game was structural steel. Walking to the man who had simply grunted, he again called out, "Good morning," and introduced himself. The fellow's name was Harry Black as it turned out; he said his friends called him Blacky. Murphy gave Harry Black a smile and asked him which name he should use. At that Harry Black returned the smile and said, "You can call me, Blacky, Michael." Harry Black was another electrical inspector but he was from the UK.

Now came the challenge, the guy who had said nothing. Murphy walked over to the fourth man who was leaning on a table full of prints. Murphy leaned on the table beside the man who at this point was using his hands to hold up his head. "You having a bad day, partner?" Michael ventured.

At that the man turned slowly toward Murphy. His eyes looked as if they were hanging out on celery stalks. "What?" was all he said.

Murphy repeated his good morning and extended his right hand.

Finally the man acknowledged him and made an attempt to extend his hand to shake with Murphy, grunting, "Good morning."

Michael noticed the shaking hand as the man extended it. "My name is Michael Murphy and I'm glad to meet you."

As the two men shook hands, the fellow's head slipped from the left hand which was still holding up his head. He caught himself before his head could hit the print table.

"I'm Andy Williams. Excuse me, please, I got into the piss last night."

Murphy looked at Williams and asked him if he was related to the singer.

"Depends on how much sid I drink." Sid is what they call the homemade whiskey in the Kingdom.

"So, what's your trade, Andy?" Murphy said as he persisted in the conversation.

"Tin knocker, Michael," he replied, barely able to get the words out.

"Well, I'm glad to meet you, sir," Michael heartily responded. "I'm an electrician."

Taking a seat at his print table Murphy opened up the set for the office complex. Checking the location he had an idea of where to go, out towards Dammam. He decided that today he would give this project his undivided attention, get to know the electricians and let them get to know him. At this point of the job the electricians would still be putting conduit on the metal decks, before the concrete pours. Conduits would be stubbed up for partitions and panels throughout the buildings and the main service should be in progress. After that he would only have to monitor the temporary lights. Two hours and one lousy cup of coffee later Murphy was ready to go out into the field.

The directions to the job site were as he figured; he was on the highway to Dammam. The roads were now very busy and one had to be very careful at each and every intersection. As always the sky was cloudless, the road was lined with palm trees and plastic bags, and yes, the pickups hauling camels. Suddenly off to his left he spotted a grand site. A huge American flag flew out over all the palm trees: the American Embassy. The sight of the American flag made him feel good, real good.

Entering the job site was no different than any site he had ever been on. Each trade had its own lay down area and change shacks. Lay down areas are for the tools and material that will be used for the project. Change shacks are for lunch and breaks, if they in fact have either. Near the change shacks you can usually find the office manager's trailer. With his trailer near the change shacks he always knows who may be abusing their privileges.

After parking his pickup Murphy headed for the superintendent's office to check in. He found the office was empty but there were requests for inspections of two areas in his mail drop. While going over the requests the door opened and a man so big that he had to duck his head to clear the door frame entered.

"You must be Murphy, our new electrical inspector," came the words from the huge guy.

Murphy answered instantly that he was correct. He wanted to add to that, "and you must be Paul Bunyan," but thought better of it.

"Glad to make your acquaintance, Murphy, I'm Jim Stearns."

Pleased at his friendliness, Michael replied, "Happy to meet you, too, Jim."

"Do you have time enough to inspect today, Murphy?" Stearns said, considering the heavy workload.

"Yup, that's what I'm here for, Jim." Michael was glad to see that things were running smoothly and his services were indeed needed.

"Smashing, then." Jim thought having another man to work on the projects was definitely helpful.

Jim Stearns was a Brit. Figuratively speaking, he was a mountain of a man. Murphy surmised he was about six foot- nine or ten. He couldn't be sure how many stones the man went but in pounds, two hundred and sixty might be close. When he removed his hard hat Murphy's next thought was, Mr. Clean. Stearns' head was completely shaved and man, did it shine. But then again that may have been because the ceiling lights were so close to the top of his head!

Jim offered, "Would you like me to show you around, Murphy, or would you prefer to walk about on your own?"

Being familiar with the routine, Michael told Stearns, "I'll give it a go on my own, Jim, and report back when I'm done."

Murphy spent three hours walking the job. The work which had been done to date looked very good. All the conduit was secured to the rebar and the stubups were secure and capped to prevent cement from entering during the pour. The men doing the work watched Murphy as hard as he looked at their work. Most of the men were from the Philippines but a few were Indians. Michael Murphy learned years ago that these men did their work as well as the men and women he had worked with in the States; some did it even better.

Rather than talk to the men in the field, he spoke only to their foreman; it's a show of respect. There would be plenty of time to meet the crew another time. After a stop at Jim Stearns' trailer, Murphy headed back to the office in Dhahran. Stearns had been glad to hear that the inspection went well, and had also inquired about the possibility of an inspection on Thursday; that meant overtime.

"Whatever it takes, Jim, whatever it takes."

By the time Murphy had his eight hours in he was ready for a nap at the compound. Perhaps the meal would be something he would recognize; as Jim Stearns would say, "smashing."

JOAN'S FIRST CALL

Sunday was a repeat of Saturday with the exception of which project Murphy would visit, and then there was Joan's first phone call. The day went well as far as inspection of the housing project was concerned. Murphy was back at his office in Dhahran by three in the afternoon; he always worried about missing his wife's call. At three-thirty Murphy's phone rang and the receiver was up to his ear in less than one full ring.

"Inspections, Michael Murphy speaking," was the rapid greeting.

In a hushed tone came, "Hi." That was all he heard.

"Hello, Sugar, how are you?" In the back of his mind he was hoping this would be a good call.

Joan seemed so far away. "I'm good, how about you? Are you over your jet lag yet?"

"Well, it went better than I was expecting; I was back on schedule by yesterday." It seemed that both of them were keeping the conversation deliberately light.

Continuing with menial chat, Joan went on, "Did Larry meet you at the airport?"

Michael wanted to say more, but wasn't sure of his footing, "Like clockwork, Joan."

"I'm sure."

"So, what do you hear from the kids?" Murphy felt like he was pulling teeth.

"They're good and send their love," Joan sincerely spoke.

Murphy paused for a moment. "Anybody call since I left?"

"You had a call from, hold on, Chris Brown. He called on Friday, I think."

"What's up with him?" he said casually.

"Said he was sorry he missed you and said you could call him at your convenience."

Murphy didn't ask anymore about Brown's call; he made light of it and just went on. "How was your weekend?"

"It was good. I went to church with my mother and sister, then we went out to breakfast."

"I hope your breakfast was better than the slop I get here," Michael offered.

"That was your decision, pal," came her rather sarcastic answer.

Another pause. Ignoring her tone, he said, "I do have some good news for you, Sugar."

"What's that?"

"You see, my projects have to be done in six months or less." Murphy thought this rather short stay away from home might appease Joan somewhat.

Still talking with an attitude, Joan commented, "Sure, I'll believe that when I see you home. And of course this is your last trip."

Murphy needed to change the subject and fast. "How 'bout those Jets, Joan?"

To which she spit out, "Michael, you are so full of shit!"

Murphy knew he was in trouble, as usual. "Joan, please. It's hard enough here."

Joan continued, "At least I can take a shower again; the bathroom works well. If I want something done around here, all I have to do is let you go on some overseas job."

"Come on, Joan, please." Michael was beginning to wonder how this call was going to end.

But she really didn't want to have words with her husband, so far away. "Have you run into anybody you used to work with?"

"Not yet. I'm working out of the Dhahran office and with any luck that's where I am going to stay. I have a mosque on my list, Joan."

Incredulously, she said, "A mosque?"

"That's exactly what I said when Larry assigned me the project." Murphy was relieved that at least their discussion was on a little safer ground.

"You'd better be careful, Michael." Christians in this part of the world were sometimes not too well received.

He thought: "concern;" that felt good.

Thirty minutes went by and the conversation mellowed out. While Murphy knew his lifestyle made his wife crazy, he also believed she did love him; well anyway, he hoped she did.

After they said their goodbyes and hung up, Murphy sat back and thought about their call. All and all it went well. It had never been easy and without the kids to break up any tension, it still was not bad.

Next Murphy thought about Brown's call. There was no use to call him at this time since nothing had been firmed up. Maybe next week he would have something substantial to report. He didn't want to bother Peter and Paul with questions about their search although it was always on his mind. Perhaps they needed some incentive, in which case he knew just what to do. Tomorrow would be incentive day, he thought, and with that he called it a day.

COMPLETION OF WEEK ONE

Monday, Tuesday, and Wednesday of week number one went well. Murphy's projects seemed to be on cruise with some of the best manpower in the Kingdom doing the installations. He had decided on Monday to wait on his incentive promotion until Wednesday afternoon. Tuesday he made an arrangement to borrow a pair of bolt cutters from the foreman on the housing project: his investigation of the second yacht would require cutting the lock on the companionway. No questions were asked and he didn't volunteer any reason for needing the tool.

Murphy arrived at his office Wednesday afternoon. He would fill in his log and inspection request forms which were completed. Checking his mailbox Murphy found only one request form for Thursday, the office complex. The electricians had started installing conduit in the ceilings and that usually went well. Murphy would ride along on top of a scaffold which one or two electricians would push. At his signal they would stop in order for him to inspect the pipe runs and junction box installations.

If he arrived on the site by seven a.m. he could blitz and blow. Blitz and blow is the term used when one attacks the task, completes the task, and heads for home. In the States the term means a shorter than usual day but with a full day's pay. For Murphy it would mean being done by nine o'clock, maybe as early as eight-thirty.

Peter and Paul were their usual effervescent selves. As always they would laugh at the slightest thing Murphy or anybody would say. They wanted to know how Mr. Michael's week went and was there anything he may need. They inquired about Mr. Larry, since he had been so busy that they had not seen him in two days. Murphy laughed and simply said,

"My motto is, let sleeping dogs lie." After looking at each other for a second they started laughing once again.

"Enough of this small talk guys, let me ask you something. Have you had any luck finding Fozi?"

Peter was the first to speak. "It's not going well, Mr. Michael. I made two calls Monday and one Tuesday."

Paul followed up with the same type of answer. "I made a call to my brother and although he is trying to help, nothing yet so far, Mr. Michael."

Murphy thanked the guys for staying with it. He excused himself and said he would be right back. Upon his return he was carrying a package which he set on Peter's desk.

"What is this, Mr. Michael?"

"This is for you guys, your help is appreciated, and I know of no better way to say thank you."

When Peter opened the package, his eyes lit up and an ear-to-ear smile came over his face.

"Mr. Michael, 501s, Levi's, Oh, Mr. Michael."

The one thing Filipino men would kill for was Levi's, 501s especially. Peter pulled three pairs from the opened package and his smile only got bigger.

"You'd better check the sizes before you get too excited, Peter. I hope they fit." Murphy knew he had hit the jackpot.

Inspecting the labels on the back of each pair, virtually beaming, Peter commented, "They are fine, sir!"

Michael added, "One pair is for Paul, you know."

Upon hearing that, Paul's smile widened, "Oh, thank you, Mr. Michael."

"You see that there are three different sizes there, right?"

"Oh yes, sir, these will fit me and the others will fit Paul."

Murphy looked at Paul. "If neither of you can fit into the other pair, you can sell them and split the money. Perhaps your brother will fit into them, Paul."

"Don't worry, Mr. Michael, we will find someone they will fit."

"If things work out I'll see if I can get some more shipped in from home," Michael said hopefully.

Both Filipino men said in chorus, "Things will work out, sir, not to worry. You go ahead and send for more."

Murphy laughed and smiled, "I knew you would say that."

"We shall try over the weekend, Mr. Michael." Peter assured Murphy that it was only a matter of time.

Leaving the office Murphy headed out to his pickup. One thing for sure; he'd made their day.

SURVEY OF THE SECOND YACHT

Thursday morning Murphy did everything in the double-time mode. Breakfast was toast and orange juice followed by a bowl of Kellogg's Corn Flakes with a cup of nasty coffee to go. Thinking back he could not remember if the guy at the check-in desk had even seen him, as he was wrapped up in the newspaper and Murphy had breezed by. Oh, well.

The inspection didn't go as well as he had hoped it would. Out of ten locations Murphy had stopped at in the ceiling check, he found four problems. The way Murphy worked his inspections was simple. Out of ten stops he would buy two problems; however, anything over two and he would cancel the inspection. He would also ask the foreman not to embarrass him again like this, saying something like, "Please call me when your work is done in a workman-like manner."
Once a company knew how an inspector worked they would never take a chance on not being ready for him. One warning was usually enough. The inspection was done by eight-ten and Murphy was on his way to the beach.

Being early once again got him through the gate and to the beach with plenty of time to row Dick's inflatable. One thing he had not counted on was the guard's awareness of the hour. The skinny guard did his walk about the pickup and then asked Murphy why he was always there so early. Murphy was taken by surprise at this question; most guards treat you like a bother never keeping track of time and the like. "I like to run in the sand, sir, before we sail, exercise." The guard looked at Murphy, like a once over, then waved him through. As Murphy cleared the raised gate he thought to himself: can't be early tomorrow.

After getting the inflatable ready and to the water Murphy did his usual check of the beach and parking lot: all clear. The wind was light and the row out was easy. Inspection of the outside row showed no change with the only yacht he liked still there. Moving into the second row it hit him, he had forgotten the bolt cutters: what a dumb shit. After taking fifteen minutes for another trip out and back, thank God the guard had not asked him to get out of the truck so he could inspect behind the seat.

Checking the shoreline and parking lot again he climbed over the side of the yacht, reaching back to grab the bolt cutters that he had forgotten yet again. Cutting the lock off was easy, definitely not a master lock, he thought. He was going to save the lock, put it back once he was done, so it looked the same from a distance. Throw it away was his second thought, letting the owner think he forgot to put it on. Pushing the companionway hatch back and removing the hatch boards was easy also, no swelling of the wood.

Sliding down into the cabin was done feet first this time; he still had a lump on his head from last week's break in. The sails were folded up neatly forward on the V berth. On the port side settee sat the whisker pole, for holding spinnaker sails. There was canned soup in the pantry over the sink, bottled water also. Turning the selector switch on the instrument panel to the right battery bank, the amp meter showed in the green. Switching to the left battery bank, it was in the green again. Neither battery was strong high on the green line, but green is green.

Removing the engine cover Murphy was happy to see something he recognized, an Atomic Four engine. These engines are used by boat builders around the world and are very dependable. There was only one drawback as far as he could tell: the Atomic Four is a gas engine. Murphy's fear of having gas on board had always stopped him from owning one. Dependable or not, he was afraid of gas. Murphy had only three fears that he could think of in sailing: being attacked by a whale, having a whale breach next to his boat and gas. He had never known anyone who had a problem with gas fires, so he knew at some point he would have to get over it.

A check of the bilge showed no water to speak of; this is always something to be glad about. The deck board for the bilge inspection came out with no trouble at all, another good sign. The yacht had classic lines as he remembered, which should mean a full keel. In bad weather a full keel is the only way to go, very stable. A further examination of compartments under the settees proved fruitful: a crank to start the engine in case of battery failure and an emergency tiller handle. The tiller handle indicated cable steering, no problem if a cable let go.

Murphy liked everything about this yacht; it was almost too good to be true. Suddenly he remembered he had not checked the shore in some time. A look through the port holes proved useless due to other boats being in the way. Poking his head up through the companionway, Murphy almost shit! He counted six cars and someone had even set up a catamaran already. Climbing up into the cockpit of the yacht Murphy replaced the hatch boards. Slowly he pulled the companionway hatch cover over the hatch boards until the hasp plate penetrated the top hatch board. Forget the lock he thought, it's gone anyway.

Peeking towards shore one last time it was evident that no one was interested in what was going on in the mooring fleet. Staying as low as he could Murphy slid himself over the side of the yacht and into the inflatable. Shit! The fucking bolt cutter, he did it again. Staying low and moving slow Murphy reached into the cockpit deck; grasping the elusive bolt cutters once again, Murphy slid back into the inflatable. Untying from the cleat Murphy began rowing down the mooring line and rounding the end of the fleet, he headed back towards shore. He had already come to the conclusion that today's find was truly the one. The yacht on the outside row would be the back up since it had no engine.

For the next three weeks Murphy would check both yachts for any sign of use. He would row every morning before the races but his arrival time would change, later is better. Should things go in his favor he would not board the yachts for another inspection for four weeks.

It was getting close to the time he would have to call Chris Brown. The DVD Chris made would have to be sent to him soon and Marie Al Fozie would have to be contacted soon also. Murphy was thinking she may be due for a trip to Bahrain. Murphy's next thought was the child. This was the part that made him nervous. Finding the child and getting her to trust him, could he pull that off?

THREE WEEKS LATER

Michael Murphy's life in Saudi Arabia had fallen into place once again. Compound life, shopping at the gold stores with Larry, daily electrical inspections, dinner once a week with Larry and the other inspectors, off the compound, and thank God, sailing with Dick. The project that he still could not get over, the Mosque, was going well. It was located on a pump station near the edge of town, workers spending twenty-four hours on and twenty-four hours off, like fire fighters. Due to the location Murphy had to enter the site through an official guard shack. These guys did everything but pull the seat out of the truck.

One day while Murphy was standing outside his pickup, during the guards' inspection, he offered the second guard some candy. At first the guard reached for the candy and Murphy detected a smile. Suddenly the guard pulled his hand back and the smile was gone. Shaking his hand back and forth and nodding his head no, the guard refused the candy. Wondering what made the guard change his mind Murphy inquired. At that, the first guard called to Murphy, "You used your left hand, the one you wipe yourself with." Murphy knew there was no need to offer the first guard candy today either, maybe next time and remember to use the right hand.

The second incident was at the same gate, different set of guards. Murphy pulled up to the gate, opened the door to his pickup and got out. The guard who was to check the pickup walked over to Murphy for passport inspection. It was at this point that Murphy always waited for the guard to say, "Are your papers in order," but that was a different movie.

The guard had his hands full as he approached: a bottle of Pepsi was in his right hand, a machine gun in his left hand. Placing both items on the roof of Murphy's pickup he went over the papers. Handing the passport back to Murphy the guard leaned into the pickup and pulling the seat forward, he inspected behind it. For some reason he ran his hand under the back of the seat. Murphy suddenly flashed back on the bolt cutters; that's where he had put them. On second thought he remembered returning them, thank you, Lord. He was then told to open the passenger side door and stand aside; he did. The guard continued: behind the seat, under the seat, glove compartment, under the mats, above the sun visors, and last but not least, a mirror was used to look under the truck.

Murphy was instructed to get back into the pickup and then the guard closed the door. As Murphy thanked him, the guard motioned Murphy to proceed through the gate. Putting his pickup in first gear Murphy let the clutch out slowly but just as the truck began to move away from the guard shack, the yelling started. Not wanting any problems Murphy brought the truck to a stop about fifty feet from the gate. The guard in the shack, obviously very upset, was yelling something at the guard who had done the inspection.

Watching the action in the rearview mirror Murphy was still not sure what was going on. The guard being yelled at started walking toward Murphy's truck. It was then that Murphy remembered the machine gun and the soda that had been placed on the roof of his pickup. The guard reached for the items on the roof, then another motion through, with Murphy again putting his truck in gear and letting out the clutch.

Again the yelling started, this time really loud. What now? Murphy thought as he brought his pickup to a stop. Checking his rearview mirror again it hit him: the guard picked up the Pepsi and left the machine gun on the roof. As the guard made his way to the pickup for the second time the yelling continued. Embarrassed, the guard reached for the machine gun and waved Murphy through. As Murphy drove away for the third time he had a thought, what a great Pepsi commercial.

His weekend sailing continued and to date neither yacht had been moved, as far as he could tell. He got Dick to run the catamaran down the mooring line one day as they were getting ready to race. Standing on one hull he observed that the lock he had cut was not replaced; this had to be the one he would take for the passage to Bahrain.

Murphy arrived at his office to start his fourth full week. Making his way back to his print table he realized he was alone. Saturdays were hard since they were really our Mondays. There was a piece of sticky paper in the center of the prints with an instruction, "Mr. Michael, need to see you, ASAP., Peter."

Within an hour the office was buzzing. Peter and Paul were hard at it when Murphy stopped by their desks. "What's up, Peter?" Murphy inquired.

"Oh, Mr. Michael, we found your friend." Peter was beside himself.

Happily surprised, Murphy could not believe his ears. He wasn't prepared for this news so soon.
"You guys are the best!" Michael expressed his pleasure at their report.

"Sorry it took so long, Mr. Michael. He is with Star Gas now; my cousin works in his office."

"You didn't tell your cousin about the surprise, did you?"

"No, sir." Peter said emphatically.

"Well, then I guess I better tell you some good news too, little buddy." Michael coyly went on.

Anxiously awaiting the information, Peter pressed Murphy, "What could that be, please, Mr. Michael?"

Murphy was glad to tell them, "You see, I got a package for you guys Wednesday night; your timing is great. I'll bring it with me tomorrow morning. One problem though, the sizes are the same."

"Really, Mr. Michael, that's no problem."

THE STAKEOUT

Sunday morning Murphy made a slight detour on his way to work. Star Gas was a small company that dealt in propane tanks, suitable for home or commercial use. The parking lot was not secured and that made life a bit simpler. There were a number of cars in the parking lot with two of them having Jesus Fish on the back bumpers. There was a yard behind the office where trucks and holding tanks were stored. He knew that this fellow Fozi would not be driving a truck so the parking lot was all he should have to watch. He needed a way to make this simple. He needed two things: someone to point out the vehicle and what time the office closed.

The look on Peter and Paul's face when he handed them the next package was just what he thought it would be: ear-to-ear smiles once again. As they opened the package Murphy ran an idea by them: "How about we give your cousin a pair of the Levi's?"

They looked at each other and the smiles went away. "I guess we could do that, Mr. Michael, he would like that." Murphy could see they were both choking on the words Peter had just said. Levi's are something one just doesn't give up that easy. Murphy could see their discomfort. "If you would rather we give him something else, that's alright with me." With that, the smiles came back. "See what time his office closes and I could stop by. Tell him I could meet him in the parking lot when he leaves for home."

Peter told Murphy that his cousin was picked up every afternoon and given a ride to his apartment. "That's even better, Peter, I can give him a ride; two birds with one stone," came Michael's next words.

The Filipinos were obviously confused. "Two birds, Mr. Michael?"

Murphy forgot about slang. "Just give him a call and let me know what time is good for him. What's your cousin's name, Peter?

"It's Charlie, sir."

Murphy told Peter to leave a message at the project office that he would be there after lunch for an inspection.

"Yes sir, Mr. Michael, I will call him at coffee break."

When Murphy arrived at the office complex for his inspection there was a note in his mailbox. Called Charlie and he is done at four o'clock. Told him, mum's the word. Murphy had a thought: they seem to know some slang after all.

At five minutes to four Murphy pulled into the Star Gas parking lot. Most of the cars were still there although one of the cars with the fish was missing. He had barely shut his pickup down when one of the front doors opened. A young man bounced down the three front steps weighing all of one hundred pounds. White shirt, blue pants, blue tie, black shoes and jet black hair, piled high. The outfit must be universal for all office workers in the Kingdom. When he walked directly to Murphy's pickup and smiled, Michael assumed it to be Charlie.

"You are Mr. Michael?"

Murphy was happy to see him. "That's me. You must be Charlie, I assume?"

"Yes sir, that me," Charlie confirmed.

With the introductions behind them, Michael smiled, saying, "Jump in partner, where are we headed?"

142

"Downtown, sir, Hommel Street."

Murphy started his pickup and putting it in reverse said, "You've got it, Charlie." After backing out of his parking space Murphy put his truck in neutral and paused for a moment and took a chance. "Is Fozi still here Charlie?"

"Yes sir." Charlie was very respectful.

Looking at one of the Chevys Murphy inquired, "Is that his Caprice, Charlie?

"No sir, that's his Caprice over there." Michael thought: good guess on the make.

Michael pursued the topic, "Didn't he have a blue Caprice, Charlie?"

"No sir, that's the only one I have ever seen him with, the gray one." Charlie seemed very sure of himself.

Murphy felt he had to convince Charlie that he knew Fozi well and that this line of questioning was legitimate. "When I call him I must remember to ask him what happened to the blue one." Murphy took notice of the plate; he would write it down after he dropped off Charlie.

Arriving at Charlie's apartment, Murphy handed Charlie the equivalent of a twenty dollar bill. Charlie had an even bigger smile than Peter or Paul. His joy at this offering was evident, "Wow, thank you, sir."

"Thank you, Charlie. Now remember, mum's the word."

Charlie definitely wouldn't spill the beans. "Mum, yes sir."

"I want to surprise Fozi and one of the other guys at work with a party. I can't wait to see the look on their faces, Charlie." Murphy tried to smile as broadly as Peter or Paul but it didn't work nearly as well, he thought.

After Charlie closed the door to the pickup and walked toward his apartment, the false smile quickly left Murphy's face. He would race back to the Star Gas office in hopes of catching Fozi before he left for the night.

Murphy approached the parking lot but he was too late; Fozi's space was empty. He would have to wait until tomorrow afternoon to continue his surveillance. His mind started working overtime: I have to call Chris Brown. He will have to call Marie Al Fozi, and the DVD would have to be sent to him as soon as possible. The DVD: how was he going to get that into the Kingdom? He knew he should not have the DVD mailed to the Rezayat: someone may go through it as they did in Yambu. Depending on how fast he could locate the child, a date was going to have to be made, a date for the getaway.

THE STAKEOUT, DAY TWO

Monday afternoon found Murphy speeding back to Dhahran. Since everyone else was doing the same he blended right in. While many Arabs merely slow down for intersections once you get back into the city proper, Murphy had his limits. By the time he reached the Star Gas parking lot it was four o'clock, straight up. He parked his pickup about one hundred feet in front of the office entrance, a good vantage point. Within ten minutes a car pulled into the lot. Charlie, Peter's cousin, exited the front door and the game was on.

Forty-five minutes passed before a steady stream of employees followed Charlie's lead. It seemed like an eternity before someone walked over to the gray Caprice. I got him, Murphy thought. The man was dressed in western clothes, slacks and a sport shirt. He looked to be about five-ten or eleven, a bit overweight. His complexion gave the appearance of a well-tanned man, although many Arabs fit this description and can pass for Westerners. No one stopped to chat or even wave goodbye as they got into their automobiles; it was truly the end of the workday.

As Fozi drove from the parking lot Murphy started his pickup. The first problem encountered was that Fozi turned in the direction Murphy had come from. As he drove past Murphy's truck he seemed to be fooling with his radio or AC controls. Checking both ways, Murphy executed a perfect U-turn and fell in line behind the gray Caprice. Not wanting to call any attention to himself, Murphy let the distance between them open to five or six car lengths. Murphy could feel his hands begin to sweat due to the grip he had on the wheel. He reached for the AC controls and rolled up his window; relax man, relax.

Fozi's first stop was at a grocery store not five blocks from his office. Murphy debated as to whether he should follow him in for a closer look but then decided not to. After a few minutes he realized that not just his hands were sweating; he could not relax. The twenty minutes that it took Fozi to do his shopping seemed like an eternity.

Once again the gray Caprice was on the road followed by Murphy's pickup. As they neared the outskirts of Dhahran, Fozi finally turned onto a street that was lined with typical Arab homes. Most are poured cement walls, two stories with rebar sticking out of the parapet. The unfinished look is supposed to have something to do with taxes. Windows are set back in the walls which appear to be some twelve inches thick. Main doors are massive and wooden. Parking in front of the third house on the right, Fozi got out. Watching him reach back for his grocery bag, Murphy reflected that the bag looked just like the type that lined the highways around town.

Murphy continued past the house as Fozi entered; that was enough intrigue for one day. Making his way around the block he took mental notes of the area: Madinah Road was where the Fozi residence was located, the number didn't matter.

Murphy knew he should now wait until Thursday to continue the stakeout: Saturday, our time.

THE STAKEOUT, DAY THREE

Thursday morning Michael Murphy was both excited and nervous at the same time. All week this day had been on his mind and it was beginning to affect his sleep. If all went anywhere near well he would have Joan contact Chris Brown after their Sunday call. Brown should be prepared for a call on Monday morning, his time.

Parking at the end of Fozi's street at eight in the morning he planned to watch and hope for some movement within an hour or so. Instead of drinking coffee at the compound Murphy opted to carry a thermos bottle. He knew he would need the coffee but he didn't want to have to relieve himself five times before nine o'clock. At his age coffee seemed to go right through if taken in large doses.

Two hours passed with no sign of movement from Fozi's home. At eleven fifteen, one hour and fifteen minutes later, Fozi emerged. He was dressed in a trob, not Western clothes. There was a woman in black, of course, and three children: it looked like two boys and a girl. Murphy was even more excited now than he had anticipated. If this is Marie, oh, God, how lucky could I be! The family filled the gray Caprice with Fozi starting the car and off they went.

Murphy's cell phone rang just as he started his truck. Who could this be? "Hello, Murphy here."

"Michael, where are you, man?" the voice instantly sounding familiar.

Knowing immediately it was Smith, he said, "Dick, I'm sorry, I forgot to call you last night. I have to work today; man, I'm sorry I can't crew for you."

Dick Smith followed up, "Michael, you have been acting awfully strange lately, are you OK?"

At that time Fozi's car pulled out onto the main street and thankfully went in the direction that Murphy was facing. Murphy put his pickup in first and pulled out behind him, driving at a safe distance, of course. "I'm OK, Dick, really. I just have a lot on my mind but believe me I'm okay." Now Murphy was trying to shift, steer and talk on the phone at the same time. "Dick, I'm going to have to call you back; I'm in a meeting right now."

Throwing the phone to the seat Murphy grabbed the stick and caught third gear thinking, "Wow, this is easy with two hands."

Murphy followed Fozi and his family toward town staying at a safe distance. Much to his surprise the gray Caprice pulled into McDonald's parking lot. Damn, Murphy thought, I can't get anywhere close to them in a McDonald's. In the Kingdom, in all restaurants, families were separated from single men into two distinct sections. As it turned out, to his benefit there was a space empty next to the Fozi vehicle so Murphy took it. He knew he needed to have a reason for Fozi to stop. Contemplating his next move, it hit him.

He was parked on the passenger side of Fozi's car but still couldn't get a look at the little girl in the back. Simultaneously as the passenger side door opened, Murphy opened his door. The doors cleared each other, giving Murphy his chance. Faking a slip, Murphy fell to the ground between the two vehicles. Fozi's wife immediately yelled to her husband but offered no help.

Fozi raced around the back of his car and then between them. Leaning down over Murphy he asked him if he was alright, thankfully not recognizing Michael. It seems he knew instinctively to speak English. Murphy rolled over on his side and grimaced saying, "I think so." After a short time, Fozi asked if he could help him up. "Thank you," Murphy replied, accepting the help. As the man lifted Murphy to his feet he asked if anything hurt due to being raised.

"No, I'll be alright; I just need a minute." As Fozi began dusting off Murphy, Michael began to feel guilty. This guy is helping me and I'm trying to kidnap his daughter. Fozi's family gathered around Murphy while he continued to clean him off. "Can I get you some water, sir?

Murphy couldn't take it any longer. "No, really, I'll be fine, but thank you very much."

Then something happened that made Murphy feel even worse. The little girl reached over and picked up the phone that Murphy had thrown on the seat. Somehow he must have dragged it out when he faked the fall. Looking into the child's eyes, seeing her this close, he knew it was Marie. When the child went to hand the phone to Murphy, Fozi promptly grabbed the phone from the little girl's hand and handed it himself to Murphy.

Another "Thank you, sir" from Murphy and it was almost over. Murphy glanced at the little girl and thanked her also. The child looked at Murphy and said, "You're welcome, sir." At that, the woman quickly placed her hands on the child's shoulders and directed her toward McDonald's. Something was being said to Marie but Murphy could not hear.

Fozi and the two young boys followed after the woman and the little girl. Murphy caught himself shaking after he sat down in his truck and attempted to pour a cup of coffee. He also needed to take a leak.

Somewhat distraught, he decided he was done for today; he just wanted to go back to the compound and think this through. Next Saturday he would tail Fozi again but tomorrow he would spend the day sailing.

THE SUNDAY CALL

A good rest on Thursday was followed by a good race on Friday with Dick Smith. Saturday, the first day of the work week, went well. While inspecting at the office complex Murphy noticed that something was missing. He was in a conversation with the area foreman when he realized there was only one dog in the pen next to the office. He thought it unusual that the foreman had dogs on the site to start with.

One thing you don't see too often in the Kingdom is dogs. He could only remember one incident while riding his bicycle where he had seen canines. He was riding near the outskirts of Dhahran when a pack of wild dogs came out of nowhere. He pulled both brakes and jumped off leaving the bicycle between him and the dogs. Dropping the bike he then pulled his sailing knife out, opened the blade and the marlin spike, then went for the dogs. Many years before he learned that you can't run from dogs; whatever you do, you can't let them see your back.

"So, Philip, where did the rest of the dogs go?"

Philip looked at Murphy and smiled. Murphy didn't understand.

"Did you find them homes?" Murphy asked.

Philip continued to smile. "Oh, yes, sir." Philip began to rub his stomach and his smile got bigger.

It was only then that it dawned on Murphy. "You ate them?"

"Oh, yes, sir, Mr. Michael." This was upsetting to Michael, but Philip seemed very pleased with himself.

"Why did I ask?" Murphy thought to himself. Being a dog lover it was more than he could fathom. This was one of the things a person has to accept when one leaves the USA.

Philip continued, "Mr. Michael, the black dogs make you, you know, sir." At that point he raised his right hand and began moving his forefinger around and around. Going on, he said, "It makes you hard, Mr. Michael."

"Okay, Philip, I get it." On that note Murphy was ready to head out; he couldn't take any more.

By the time he returned to his office it was nearly four o'clock. Joan's call generally came in at four o'clock sharp. In most cases when the call was right on time, it meant good news.

Answering the ringing phone, Michael greeted the caller, "Electrical, Murphy here."

"Hi, Michael, how are you?" Murphy sure was happy to hear her voice.

"I'm good, Joan, how are you?"

"I'm good, too, but I would be better if you were here, Michael."

Murphy sighed, knowing right away that this conversation might be strained. "I'm going to be home before you know it, sugar."

"Right."

However to his pleasant surprise, the call actually was favorable in tone and lasted about thirty minutes. Knowing he had to get a message to

Chris Brown, Murphy waited until the last minute, so as not to turn their chat sour.

Hesitantly, he began, "Could you do me one thing, Joan?"

"What's that?" Joan responded somewhat cautiously.

"Call Chris Brown and let him know I will call him tomorrow morning at eight-thirty." Murphy blurted out.

"Michael, really, what's that all about?" Joan clearly was exasperated.

"Please, Joan, can you just give him that message. Don't leave him a message on a machine; you have to tell him personally, eight-thirty, in the morning. If you can't contact him, call me back leaving a message on my machine. "

Sounding rather defeated, Joan went on, "Okay, Michael, is his number in our book?"

"It is. Call his home phone if you have to. If I don't hear from you I will assume you got him." Murphy's plan was on track.

"Sure, Michael, but you do know what assume means, Michael?" she countered in a somewhat mocking tone.

Thinking she had called him much worse in the past than that, Michael replied, "Very funny, Joan."

After their goodbye Murphy sat there staring out of his office window. Next, the DVD would have to be mailed to his compound, no, his office. Marie Al Fozi would have to prepare herself; she would be flying to Bahrain on short notice. Once in Bahrain she would have to get a hotel room and be prepared to stay at least a week. She would require a passport for her daughter but it would need to show the child's entry into

Bahrain. He had no idea how he would be able to pull off the passport part.

Startling him, Murphy's phone rang. Reaching for it he could see and feel his hand shake. "Electrical, Murphy speaking."

"What am I, a piece of shit?" came a booming voice at the other end.

"Laurence, what's up?" Michael was greatly relieved it was Larry and not Joan. Murphy was feeling good that he had this friend, when Larry went on, "How about dinner, you worm?"

Quickly accepting the invitation, Michael said, "Sounds good partner."

"Good, how 'bout six o'clock; that okay with you, Michael?"

"I like it." In the back of his mind Murphy was thinking about letting Larry in on his scheme. On second thought, not yet, he warned himself.

Deep in his thoughts, Michael almost didn't hear Larry say, "See you at the Rezayat then."

"OK, Larry, sounds great."

Murphy hung up. He was glad Larry had called since he was starting to zone. If nothing else, Larry had changed his mood.

MONDAY MORNING CALL

Dinner with Kelly was just what the doctor ordered. It was like having a meal with Lou Costello, never knowing what to expect, and Kelly even looked a little like him. Kelly was satisfied with the way things were going on the projects that he had assigned Murphy. He even attempted to give Murphy one more project, however, that didn't fly.

Out of the blue Kelly mentioned how Peter and Paul were so excited to have the new Levi's. "How did you come up with that idea?" he asked. Murphy smiled and said, "I was taught by the best, Larry." Kelly then smiled, remembering how many pairs of jeans he had used for favors. "Just don't spoil the boys on me, Michael. I haven't done anything like that for them in a coon's age."

Monday afternoon Murphy sat at his desk and dialed Chris Brown's office. There it was: that shaking in his hand again. He managed to get the number dialed in spite of his nerves. As the phone began to ring Murphy tried to relax.

"Brown and Brown, good morning," came a responsive voice.

Short and sweet, "Hi, Chris, it's Michael Murphy."

"Mr. Murphy, how are you?"

"I'm good, Chris. How about you?" Michael thought: enough of this small talk.

Happy to be talking to Michael finally, Chris went on, "I have to be honest with you, Michael, I'm a little nervous. How's the job coming along?"

"Everything is going fine. I saw our friend a few days ago and she's good. It's going to take a couple of more weeks before we can get together for our trip." Murphy was hedging his words.

Chris Brown could not believe what he was hearing. Five weeks had passed without a word and now out of the blue, this!

"Have you spoken to any of her relatives lately, Chris?"

"Every other day, Michael."

"Tell them not to worry. Things are going well and I anticipate our starting home in about three weeks." Murphy could hear his words as they entered the receiver and at the same time wondered how he would make this all happen.

Chris Brown was dumbfounded. "What can I do for you, Michael?"

Murphy's plan was coming together. "Send me the DVD. You have to send it to my office. But first, can you go out and find some 'Little House on the Prairie' DVDs? If you can even get three or four, that would be better. Then, somewhere in the middle of them, insert our DVD.

Brown was confused. "What in the heck are you going to do with 'Little House on the Prairie' DVDs, Michael?"

"'Little House' is the only show that is allowed to be viewed in the Kingdom, Chris, because it's wholesome. Think about it, Chris, a wholesome American show, wow! You can even have it shipped in and the mailman will deliver it." There were many other programs available but few from the U.S. Dishes were getting around but in some places they too were illegal. "So you get my drift, Chris? Lose it in the package somewhere."

"Alright, Michael. Anything else?" Chris seemed to be catching on.

"Yes, let the relatives know they will be taking a trip to Bahrain sometime in the next month." Murphy went to great lengths to be concise but thorough. He continued, "Make sure they have passports and a week to spend sightseeing. They should go on the Internet and locate a hotel, preferably by the sea. Let them know they will only have a day's notice so they should prepare their employer. Also, they need to advise you in advance which hotel they booked. Did you get all that, Chris?" Talking cryptically took some deliberation, Michael realized.

"Yes, sure did, Michael," came the retort.

Murphy remembered another point of significance to discuss with Chris. "Oh, one more thing, Chris. Will you be available at your desk for the next month, specifically at this time in the morning?"

"I'll make it my business to be here, Michael."

"Thanks, but that means Saturday and Sunday, too, Chris. Sorry to tell you that."

"No, problem, I'll be here." Chris was so deep into this plot that he knew he would do whatever was required of him.

Murphy didn't expect to be calling in the next two weeks but wanted Chris to be there anyway. The situation called for discipline; there could be no mistakes.

Murphy gave Chris the address, concluding the call.

After hanging up the phone he checked his right hand: not good, not bad.

THE STAKEOUT, DAY FOUR

Thursday morning found Murphy parked down the street from the Al Fozie residence once again. It was eight o'clock according to the Armed Forces radio station. If nothing else you got to hear some music from home. Fozi's street was quiet and the gray Caprice was parked in front of his house.

"Free Falling" played on the radio as Murphy positioned himself in the bench seat for his watch. "She's a good girl, crazy 'bout Elvis, boyfriend too." Murphy looked at the radio: he felt something was missing. "Loves Jesus, what happened to 'loves Jesus?'" When the verse repeated itself he paid close attention. "She's a good girl, crazy 'bout Elvis, boyfriend too." Wow, they censored the song and cut Jesus out of the song. What next? he thought.

Almost like clockwork Fozi came out of his house followed by the family, just after ten. As the car doors closed, Murphy had a thought: they couldn't be going to McDonald's. He started his pickup and was pleased to see Fozi head in the same direction as last week. Giving Fozi some latitude Murphy finally pulled out to follow the car. Sure enough they went straight to the land of the Big Mac, thank you, Lord, a pattern seems to be forming. He would not attempt to park near the car this week. God forbid they should recognize him. All five of them walked into the family entrance. Eventually Murphy entered the non-family entrance.

The counter help looked like the store should be in the Philippines. At first it appeared there was no way to contact someone in the other section. On closer inspection Murphy found that both sections had access to the rest rooms. The ladies room was closer to the family section so there was no reason a male should stray into the area. Murphy walked

157

up to the counter, thinking he may as well try their coffee. In order not to need a bathroom during his stakeout he had not even carried a thermos.

"May I help you, sir?" He was so deep in thought by this time that he almost didn't hear the question.

Quickly composing himself, Michael replied, "Yes, thank you. One small coffee, please."

The staff was courteous and efficient, saying, "Anything with it, sir?"

It was almost lunch or it could be if he chose, he realized after glancing at his watch. "Got any McNuggets ready?" Good 'ole McDonald's: you could always count on the consistency.

"Yes sir, how many feces?"

Michael couldn't believe his ears. "Excuse me?"

The Filipino repeated, "How many feces, sir?"

Murphy wanted to laugh. He didn't, but couldn't resist a smile. In the man's vernacular, he said, "Six, please, six feces."

For some reason he flashed back on the Pepsi incident: now we have a McDonald's incident. After he paid the man at the counter (no girls were allowed to work the counter), it was out to the pickup and off to the races. He would not be able to take part but he could at least row for awhile and be content just to be an observer.

ROW, ROW, ROW YOUR BOAT

By the time Murphy reached the Yacht Club the race was in progress. He parked near the dingy racks so people would not pay much attention to him, he thought.

So much for that premise. No sooner had he killed the engine then he heard, "Michael Murphy, where have you been?" It was Mary Smith.

Michael was always happy to see Mary, although he had hoped to slip in unnoticed. "I called, Mary, I swear."

With a slight humor in her words, "Well, due to your absence, I had to send my little girl out with Dick. I was hoping I would have one child that liked to make quilts." That was one of the pastimes for women in the Kingdom, i.e., Western women.

Apologizing profusely, Murphy, "I can't say how sorry I am, Mary."

"You know I'm only kidding, Michael; Dick's ruined all three of the girls. If any of them pick up a needle, it will be to repair a sail. So what's up with you?"

Murphy definitely felt a need for a respite. "I got done early, Mary, and thought I might at least have time to row, therapy, eh, what."

Mary and Dick enjoyed Michael's company. "Well, stop and see us after the race, Michael."

"It's a date, Mary." He was content to reply to her invitation.

After getting the inflatable prepared and over to the shore, Murphy walked it into the water and boarded. He began rowing straight for the mooring fleet thinking how good it felt to pull on the oars. As soon as he passed the outside line he let up and drifted. The wind was light and that meant the race would take longer than usual. A light breeze also meant a slow drift. Murphy stood up and let go of the oars. Placing his hands on his hips, he rocked his upper body forward, sideways, back and then forward again.

When he reached his goal, the third yacht in, he found the cockpit unchanged. The waterline was the same, the standing rigging was taut, and she had not been moved. Sitting down Murphy began rowing again. He turned up between the outside row and the next one in. Since he had to be on the other end to drift he continued rowing to windward. Reaching the windward end Murphy again let go of the oars and stood up: exercise time. Good luck smiled on Michael Murphy once again. The companionway on his first choice was still unlocked, waterline fine, rigging good and she had not been moved.

Checking the shoreline and the parking lot, Murphy saw no problems. The racing fleet was laboring in the light breeze nearly a half mile from shore. He sat down and rowed straight to the yacht in the second row. Why not board, see if anybody picks up on it. If he was questioned about boarding he would say that one of the pennants was off the bow cleat. All moorings are connected to the bow of the boat by two pieces of line known as pennants. The large float or ball in the water receives the other end of the pennants.

Tying the inflatable to the yacht, Murphy climbed into the cockpit. Walking forward he used the shrouds for balance; there were no life lines and that was not good. Making a mental note he would have to make a harness for the child. Bending over the bow he pretended to adjust the pennants. They were worn but would last as long as he would need them. Moving back to the cockpit Murphy opened the hatch and removed the hatch boards. He entered the cabin like a sailor, not head first. Checking the batteries first he found the amp reading was the same, batteries must be new he thought to himself. There was no reason for him to dally in the cabin; he had done the inventory a month before.

Back out to the cockpit, close up the companionway. Opening the starboard side bench he found only spare lines and fenders. Fenders are used when you tie up to a dock, protecting the side of the yacht from the wood or metal construction of the dock. He opened the port side bench and found what he was looking for: the gas tank. Without his glasses, and squinting, it looked like a half tank. Murphy was used to diesel, oh well.

Closing the cover Murphy stood up in the cockpit and looked around, nothing. Time to go, he thought, don't want to push my luck. Into the inflatable, untie the line, he was off. For the next hour Murphy exercised in the inflatable. Eventually the racing fleet made it back to the finish line and their day was done. For some reason he noticed that Dick Smith finished second: how could that be? Maybe the absent crew would have made a difference in their finish order?

After a picnic with the Smiths, Murphy was ready to head for the house. As it turns out, Dick got a second because he let his daughter swim for ten or fifteen minutes. Michael's balloon was burst!

THE SMUGGLING INCIDENT

Friday morning Murphy woke up to the sound of the BBC in the background. He had fallen asleep with the TV on, must have been the rowing. Feeling no discomfort in his arms and shoulders must mean that he was getting back into shape. At sixty-two he was still able to do twenty miles on his bicycle daily. Weekends he could push that to forty miles if the weather was right, the wind having a lot to do with it also.

He had two inspections to do today but that would be after breakfast. One of the Brits that Murphy worked with lived on a nearby compound. His wife was with him as was the case of many British inspectors. One day Murphy commented on how it must be nice to have home-cooked meals every day. His friend, Johnny Jones, said that having your spouse around certainly did have its advantages.

John P. Jones, P. for Peter, had invited Murphy to join them for a meal some day. It tickled Murphy that Johnny's name was similar to an American war hero. Johnny had asked Murphy what his favorite meal was. "I miss a good breakfast," was his reply. "Bacon and eggs, potatoes fried in butter on the side." Jones laughed at Murphy, "You know they don't sell bacon here in the Kingdom, Michael."

Now on Murphy's compound there were guys from all walks of life and many different types of employment. One of Murphy's buddies was a retired Air Force Load Master who worked at the airport. Military aircraft were kept at the civilian airport in Dhahran, something that always bothered Murphy.

Another worker was Sam White who was a black man in his early sixties. He was a mountain of a man at six-foot-five and three hundred pounds. There was not an ounce of fat on Sam. He was always telling stories about his service career and each was funnier than the next. Now, the military got rations of this and that while they were stationed in the Kingdom. Lo and behold, one of the items was bacon. Out of the blue, during dinner at the compound one evening, Sam asked if anyone wanted some bacon. Murphy's mouth started to water.

Astonished, Murphy almost choked on his meal. "Are you kidding, Sam?"

"No, Michael; why, are you interested?"

Michael couldn't answer quickly enough. "How much can you get?"

Sam didn't have a clue what his provisions would mean to Murphy. "How much do you want?"

Then without even thinking twice, Murphy blurted out, "Five pounds."

"I think I can do that." Sam was pleased he could help another comrade. No one else at the table seemed to be interested and Murphy now wished he had said ten pounds.

Now how it works is simple. Anyone who did not wish to receive their ration of bacon for whatever reason, could use it as a trade item. You take the bacon and trade it for something else. The long and short of it was that Sam got Murphy the five pounds of beacon, and Murphy put it in his apartment refrigerator.

A day or so later Murphy mentioned to John P. Jones that some good fortune had come his way in the form of bacon. Jones reacted the same way Murphy did when he heard about the availability of bacon. He offered to buy the bacon and give Murphy two breakfasts prepared by his wife. Murphy asked if his wife might mind him volunteering her services that way. "You just bring the bacon and then tell me what you think."

So that morning Murphy was going to collect on the promise. He decided he would not charge Jones for the treat: it would be on him. Murphy put the bacon in a sack first, then in a box, to keep it cool. Leaving the compound Murphy noticed the gate was open again, and there was no guard; more shit to complain about. The drive to the Jones' compound would take only ten minutes. He could taste the bacon already.

He had driven less than a mile when he came upon a traffic delay. There were a dozen cars waiting in line and at first Murphy thought nothing of it. As he neared the front of the line it became evident that a road block had been set up. This is nothing new although Friday was unusual, a holy day. Murphy knew to avoid large crowds on Friday. Heads were lopped off on Fridays. If a Westerner were found in a crowd, they were sometimes brought to the front. Arabs liked you to see that they do not fool around and that their justice is swift. Hands were lopped off on Fridays also. Obviously, he wanted no part of either!

Then it hit him. He was two vehicles from the road block when he thought of the bacon sitting on the seat next to him. He was transporting contraband. Guards were walking up and down the line of cars and he knew there was no time to shove the bacon under the seat. Was he going to jail for five pounds of bacon? How was he going to explain this to his office, when they came to get him out of jail? How would he explain it to Joan when he would not be there for her phone call on Sunday? How long does one get for five pounds of bacon?

Reaching the front of the line Murphy rolled down his window. "Egamma," passport, the guard said. Murphy handed it to the guard. "Where you are going?"

"I am going to work sir."

The guard grew suspicious. "On Holy day?"

Murphy rapidly responded, "Non- Muslim, sir."

Then the inevitable. "What's in the box?"

This was it, he was going to jail. In a split second Murphy had a thought. Faking a sneeze into his left hand, Murphy then reached for the box. As his left hand brought up the box to the window Murphy said, "Candy. Would you like some candy, sir?" He pushed the box out the window and repeated himself, "Please, take some."

Abruptly, the guard pulled back and shook his head no. Murphy was thinking: the ass-wipe hand with a sneeze was going to save his life. He pulled the box back into the truck. He wondered how in the world the guard did not notice how awkward it was to handle the box with his left hand. When the guard handed Murphy back his Egamma, Murphy took it with his right hand. After being waved through Murphy took a deep breath…never again.

Even when considering the ordeal, in the end, it all seemed worth it. It was the best breakfast he had eaten since England. John P. Jones and his wife laughed at Murphy. Eventually he was relaxed enough to laugh with them.

THE DVD

In the middle of the seventh week Murphy's package arrived. A thought crossed his mind...Chris has been waiting by the phone every day, perhaps tomorrow I can call him. When Peter and Paul brought the package to Murphy they were both wearing big smiles. They stood there and waited as Murphy inspected the condition of the package. When it dawned on Murphy that his two little buddies had not left, he stopped and looked up. May I do something for you, my friends?

"No sir." They didn't move, they just stood there smiling.

Murphy thought for a while. "You want to see what's in the box, don't you?"

One said, yes sir and one said no sir. Looking at each other, they now started laughing out loud.

Murphy started laughing with them. "OK, let's see what we have here."

Besides finding the box in good shape he found the contents packed neatly; when packages are checked they usually are a mess inside. As Murphy unwrapped the DVDs Peter and Paul closed in on him for a peek.

He needed some space so said, "Hey guys, give me some room here, okay?"

"Sorry, sir," they said in unison.

Murphy knew just what to say. He looked up slowly and smiled, "I think we have some porno."

That was all Peter and Paul had to hear. "Mr. Michael!" they cried.

There were four sets of DVDs. "Oh, nuts," Murphy said, 'It's "Little House on The Prairie.' You guys like 'Little House?'"

Suddenly Peter and Paul seemed to lose interest.

"You can borrow them if you like."

"That is fine, sir, but no, thank you, Mr. Michael."

Now alone, Murphy began to check each case. The third case felt different, it looked the same; this must be it Murphy thought. A close examination proved his suspicion correct. There were two DVDs in the case and one was blank. He remembered telling Chris not to mark the disk they made with Marie Al Fozi. Reaching down to his drawer he pulled out a portable DVD player. Looking around at first to see if anyone was close, he loaded the disk into the player. Pushing the play button and after a slight pause, Marie Al Fozi appeared. She was sitting in a chair and on her lap was a doll...her daughter's favorite doll. Marie had not begun to speak when Murphy had a flash, I need the doll. The doll will do it.

Checking his watch he saw that it was the middle of the night for Chris. He realized that he would have to call him at home. Looking up the home phone number was a pain in the ass. He had to get it from the address book he had in his truck. Finally he was dialing the number and after a few seconds it began to ring. The phone must have rung ten times before the receiver was lifted: he wondered why it had not gone to the machine for a message.

A sleepy voice came on, "Hello." It was Jane Brown, damn.

"Mrs. Brown, it's Michael Murphy, I'm sorry to bother you at this hour."

"Hello," came the voice a second time.

Michael tried again. "Mrs. Brown, it's Michael Murphy, may I speak to Chris?"

Noticeably annoyed, she countered, "Do you know what time it is?"

"I'm really sorry, Mrs. Brown, it's very important or I wouldn't have bothered you in the middle of the night."

Finally the voice of Chris Brown came back at Murphy. "You said eight in the morning, Michael."

Murphy was so psyched that he wasn't very concerned about their displeasure. "Sorry, Chris, after this you can sleep late. Get in touch with Marie ASAP. Tell her to give you the doll she was holding when we made the DVD. I have to have the doll and you need to send it no later than tomorrow afternoon. Fed Ex the doll, Chris. Are you there, Chris?"

"I hear you, Michael."

"Listen, Chris, tell Marie she needs to make reservations for two weeks from today. Did she inquire about hotel reservations, yet?"

"Yes, she did, Michael." Now wide awake, Chris rose up on one elbow. "Is it going to happen that soon, Michael?"

Murphy was throwing caution to the wind regarding the need for code language. "I found out that the family has a routine, every Thursday morning. I have to do it then, it's the best time."

Concerned for Michael's safety, Chris asked, "Are you okay, Michael? Are you sure you can do this?"

"The answer to your first question is, 'I'm scared shitless.' The answer to your second question is the same as the first one."

"You know that you don't have to do it, Michael, if anything goes wrong."

Frustrated, Murphy exclaimed, "Great, this is a fine time to tell me that, pal. Get that doll to my office pronto. By the way, I got the DVDs today. You did good."

"Anything else, Michael?" Chris felt so responsible and here he was safe and sound in his own bed at home in the States.

"Just make sure Marie makes her reservations. I should talk to you in a day or so. You know what…I'll call to confirm that I have the doll. And, one more thing…"

Chris was paying close attention. "What's that, Michael?"

"Tell your wife I am sorry, really; she sounded quite upset by my rudeness."

"No problem, Michael, she's sound asleep; she won't even remember that you called."

"Oh, yes she will. Go back to sleep, now and we'll talk soon. And thanks, Chris."

THE COUNTDOWN BEGINS

After Murphy hung up the phone he realized that he had just committed to a date. He set the wheels in motion that were to return the child to her mom, and he would be back with Joan.

At the end of the week Murphy's mailbox was full of inspection requests. The next package hadn't yet arrived and this meant he would have to wait until Saturday. He would call Dick Smith and beg off again on sailing. Thursday morning he would tail Fozi, before he did his inspections. Please God, make Thursday another McDonald's morning. Friday he would check the yachts for activity. If he could only confide in someone in the Kingdom; at times he felt very lonely. Sooner or later he would have to tell Larry which was going to be hard. The bottom line was bad....he had used Larry.

Murphy found a sticky-back note on his desk. It was from John P. Jones: "Can you make breakfast tomorrow? We have some great bacon, Michael. As always, John." Everything is a big joke.

The week had ended with no problems, all three projects going well. He did notice that the last dog was gone at the office complex. Kelly had been out of town for the last week on oil rigs, lots of overtime on the rigs. In the evenings Murphy studied the DVD, it being ten minutes long. When the time came he was not sure how he was going to make contact with the little girl. What's the big deal? He still had eight days to figure that out.

Tonight Murphy would go for shopping, as they say in the Kingdom. He wanted to find out if he could buy an outfit like the Arab ladies wear, perhaps a pair of heels, black and low. What he had on his mind was crazy; this was a good place to go in drag. He had to get into the ladies restroom and then somehow get the child into it, also.

Thursday was the last time he would check the Yacht Club. If nothing changes, that would be a cake walk. He did have to get the child through the gate and this might be where that large bag of his could come in handy. He was sure she would fit in it but he better double check on Thursday.

He still needed a chart of the Gulf and then there was the weather to contend with. He didn't need bad weather but he definitely didn't want good weather, either. The moon was the only thing he had kept track of: it would not be full, maybe half. Wind was a crap shoot, although he was thinking that ten to fifteen knots would be great. How would the child react to sailing? How would she react to being taken from her dad? The DVD was good but the doll was the crux of it.

Somehow he would use the doll to get her attention and lure her into the ladies restroom. Murphy reached for a cigarette; you quit smoking twenty years ago, asshole. Suddenly his phone rang.

"Electrical, Murphy."

A booming voice that was undeniably recognizable, "You mother fucker!"

Murphy uttered his typical response, "Up yours, Larry."

"So what's shacking, brother?" Larry's dialect was unique.

"I was just thinking about you, too, Larry," came Murphy's hearty comeback.

Kelly emphatically returned, "I'm not into same sex relationships, Michael."

Murphy was glad to hear from his buddy who was always good company. "Okay, Larry, how about dinner then?"

"You got it, six o'clock?" Clearly, Larry was a man of few words.

"See you there, Larry." Once again Larry Kelly had bailed him out, just when he needed a good laugh. Maybe he would come clean with his friend.

DINNER WITH LARRY

Murphy was not sure what he had just put on his plate; it was called steak. The potatoes and vegetables may have to be the main course. The dessert was some kind of pudding, yellow and with a cherry in the middle. The fellow at the door, as usual, did not look up as Murphy passed. Joining Larry at his table, Murphy emptied his tray and set it to one side.

"How's your day been, Larry?" Murphy started.

In a somewhat frustrated manner, Kelly snapped, "Michael, there's just not enough time in the day."

Michael understood. "How were the rigs?"

"One good thing out there is the food is a lot better than the shit we have to eat here." Larry didn't often mince words.

Murphy laughed. "You don't look like you've missed too many meals, Larry."

"Aw, Michael, y'know, I have feelings, too."

Michael turned serious at this point, saying, "Larry, I need to talk to you about why I took this assignment for you."

Larry knew Murphy well. "Shit, I should have realized something was up."

Regretfully, Michael told his pal that he might have to leave in about two weeks.

"Don't tell me that and then call me pal." Kelly was pissed at the news. "I'm in a bind here, Michael; if you bail on me, I'm fucked six ways to Sunday."

"Wait, hear me out, Larry. I got a call from a lawyer in New York. A client or friend of his has a big problem."

Larry was not the least bit sympathetic to the tale unfolding. "From what I'm hearing, this has created a huge problem for me, too."

Murphy was feeling worse by the minute having to unload the unpleasant circumstances on his trusting buddy. "Please, just listen. A child was taken or kidnapped, by her father. This happens to be where she is now."

"Oh, I see, so you think you can just grab her, jump on a plane, and fly back to New York, just like that?" Larry was highly doubtful.

"Come on, Larry, give me a break. It's a little more technical than that. I'm not stupid. I spent the last two months formulating a plan. I have to move soon."

"So where does that leave me? You know that'll put me in a bind. I wish you just could have told me the truth. You're into more shit than you know, Michael. If you get caught you will never see New York again. How could you let yourself get involved in something like this?"

Murphy elaborated, "I didn't go looking for trouble. They called me, Larry. I never wanted to come back here again. Sure as hell, Joan didn't want me to, either. I was happy sailing around in the Atlantic. I'll bet you would have done the exact same thing if they had called you."

"But....they didn't call me, partner, did they? They called your dumb ass. Okay, I'll make you a deal, Michael. I'll help you but you have to finish the jobs for me. How much time do you need to pull this off, and this time I want the whole sorry story."

Murphy couldn't help but smile, thinking, Larry always comes through.

Thoughtfully, Kelly remarked, "Why did you think you couldn't tell me the truth? How much shit have we been through together? You hurt my feelings real bad, Michael."

"I'm sorry Larry, it will never happen again," Michael said apologetically.

Michael Murphy spent the next hour explaining his plan to his friend. Listening intently, Larry never once spoke. "With any luck I want to do this in eight days, what do you think?"

"Michael, surely you aren't asking me what I really think? What I know is that you're fucking nuts, pal, but it just might work. I will take you and the kid to the Yacht Club since you can't leave your truck there. Leave your truck at the office. A two-week emergency leave starting next Thursday will be set up for you. Your passport will be needed in case you have a problem in Bahrain. I'll be with you at McDonald's getting some coffee and a muffin. If you do get the kid to go with you, I'll be waiting outside. And, one last issue."

Relieved that he was no longer alone in this escapade, Michael went on, "What's that, Larry?"

"Should I get you a coffee and muffin to go for you?" Larry snickered.

Murphy laughed. "And you say I'm crazy?"

"And a final thing. You have to promise me you will be back as soon as the kid is with her mother. I mean, if you want to get your horn scraped while you're over there, that's OK. But you've got to promise me that, Michael. You owe it to me."

Michael knew he was indebted to Kelly in a way that couldn't be explained. "I'll be back, Larry. I can't thank you enough for what you're doing for me, particularly considering your own risks."

"Just come back and finish your job, that's thanks enough. Come to think of it, Michael, why don't you get two blow jobs and bring me back one." Larry always had a way of making a serious situation lighthearted.

Murphy felt a warmth come over him that only good friends could experience. "You ever going to change, Larry?"

"Nope! Why should I? Now let's go for shopping; we have to find you a nice veil and abia."

SATURDAY MORNING (2)

Murphy arrived at his office early on Saturday morning. It was all he could do to stay in bed five hours. Shopping on Wednesday night went well, happening to run into Dick and Mary Smith. At some level, Michael took Mary into his confidence and she got everything he needed. She thought the clothing was for Michael to bring home to his wife, wanting to surprise her. The shoes he handled himself, size ten and a half. Larry wanted to go back to the compound and see what Murphy would look like in Arab drag. But Murphy told him he would have to wait until Thursday morning. That would be the only time Kelly would ever see him in a veil.

By nine o'clock Murphy was ready to leave the office to make his usual rounds. Peter and Paul showed up at his desk as he slid off his chair.

"Mr. Michael, you have another package, sir."

"Just leave it on the desk, guys, I may have to leave soon." One thing Murphy didn't want to do was explain the doll to his little buddies. He fumbled with some prints as they finally left. He opened the package and was happy to see that it had not been rifled before delivery. A doll might have been something that would cause suspicion, being sent to a business office. It was in fine shape for a rag doll. Murphy thought it was a good sign: his sailboat's name was Rag Doll. The doll was the size of a newborn baby. How in the devil was he going to be able to hide this until the last minute? Under the doll was an envelope. Opening it, he found a picture of Marie holding her daughter on her lap while her daughter held the doll. He thought, nice touch, Marie!

Everything seemed to be falling into place, especially since Larry had offered his help. Larry was a diamond in the rough but always a good friend. During the early nineties Murphy had been out of work for nearly six months. Larry would often call and ask him to fly to Washington State where Boeing was doing the 777 facilities. The union hall in Everett had a call out for men for weeks. Murphy was trying to hold out for a job closer to home but it never happened.

Kelly knew Murphy was financially stretched rather tight; unemployment was not cutting it. Out of the blue one day Kelly called Murphy, saying, "I'm sending you a plane ticket for this Saturday morning and two mortgage payments. See you Saturday afternoon." Having been an only child, Murphy felt that if one had a brother, this is what it would be like.

Murphy put the rag doll in his locker with the picture for safe keeping. Peter showed up for the second time, reporting, "I will have your passport ready for Wednesday, Mr. Michael. I hope everything is alright, sir."

"It will be, Peter, and thank you." He truly was so grateful for these pleasant and efficient workers.

Peter continued, "I surmise you don't need any plane tickets, sir, or is that a mistake?"

Looking at Peter, Murphy thought to himself, this guy never misses a trick. "I'm only going to Bahrain, Peter. Thanks anyway." The rest of the day Murphy would do inspections but his mind had only one thing on it: five days to go. While at the Mosque Murphy ran into an old friend, John Walsh. "How the hell are you, John?"

Elated, Walsh spoke, "Michael Murphy, I was beginning to think I would never see you again. I ask about you all the time. I tell everybody how you got me through the airport without getting arrested. I often imagine myself running into that little prick on a dark street, Michael."

Murphy advised, "Let it go, John, people like that…well, you know what I say, time wounds all heels."

Walsh looked at Murphy, bewildered for a second, then saying, "Oh, I get it Michael. Sometimes it takes me a while, though."

"So how's the welding business, partner?" Michael asked.

"Busy. This is only the second time for me to leave the shop. I have to check the dome. Somebody reported there was some concern about welds up there."

Michael was in a hurry. "John, I have to go. Do you still have Larry's number?"

"I guess I have it somewhere," came John's reply.

Murphy wrote down both numbers for Walsh. "I will be out of town for a week or so; but after that I'll call and we can set something up, a meal maybe. Good to see you, and know that you're safe."

"So long for now, Michael. Good to see you, too, and I'll look forward to getting together after you return."

With that, they were both on their respective ways.

SUNDAY - FINAL WEEK

Saturday night was hell for Murphy. He spent an hour staring at the ladies wardrobe hanging on the closet door. The shoes, could he walk in heels? Suddenly he thought of MASH, and what was that guy's name who wanted the section eight? Klinger, Max Klinger. Maybe it was spelled with a C, Clinger. He forgot to bring the rag doll home with him, still not sure how he was going to carry the damn thing. Perhaps he could tuck it under his abia, as if he were pregnant. No, Larry could never see him doing that; that wouldn't fly. Wrap it in a blanket, like a baby, nobody would pick up on that. He began to picture Larry opening the door for him.. This was going to be fun for Kelly.

Murphy faced another night of tossing and turning. Tomorrow would bring the countdown to three days and a wake up. With Larry on board he did feel somewhat relieved. But he knew he would be in for the jokes; Kelly would never let him off easy, that's for sure..

Sunday went as well as could be expected and he got back to his office in time to call Chris Brown. Dialing the number was getting easier, and this might end up being the last time he would have to do it. The ringing started and he was not shaking.

"Brown and Brown," came Chris's voice, as the phone was picked up on the first ring.

"It's Michael, Chris, good morning." The greeting always came easily, he thought.

"Mr. Murphy, how are you?" Chris waited with baited breath.

"I'm good, Chris, how about you?" Simple dialogue for two who were involved in a major conspiracy.

"Same as ever, Michael." This conversation didn't seem to be going anywhere fast.

Murphy got to the point. "I have the doll, Chris. What kind of a schedule are we looking at for Marie?"

"She will be in Bahrain Wednesday morning, Michael, and her reservations are for the Coast Hotel near the yacht basin. She explained that she needed to be within walking distance. Out of three hotels, that was the only one close enough."

"Great, Chris. What is her room number?"

"Oh, I didn't think to get that for you, Michael. Sorry." Chris felt bad at disappointing Michael.

"Don't worry. Would you just ask her to call them back and nail down a room number for me. She can fabricate some excuse for needing it, just work it out. I'll get back to you tomorrow for the answer."

"Alright, Michael, you got it. I need to ask you something, though."

"Shoot." Murphy was on a roll.

"We have never discussed a fee. Marie is concerned and so am I."

Murphy hadn't given this much thought. "I'll have to think about that, Chris. How is she fixed for money, what with the old man bailing out and all."

"I think she's in good shape, had her own money before she married."

"How much are you charging her, Chris?"

Chris thought for a minute before responding, "Actually, I don't think we ever discussed a fee, Michael."

"You don't think you have ever discussed a fee? Come on, Chris, that doesn't sound reasonable, considering that you're a professional."

"Honestly, Michael, we never have."

Murphy was astounded. "You know, your wife is going to be pissed, Chris."

"That's another thing I didn't give any thought to, either, Michael."

"Well, let me know what you decide, partner." At that point Murphy had a serious thought. "If anything goes wrong, Chris, see that my wife is taken care of. We both know I have an income already so let me think about it for a day."

"Whatever you say, Michael." Chris Brown paused for a minute." Michael, please be careful."

Murphy interrupted Chris Brown at that juncture. "Don't get sloppy on me now, Chris. I have to go. Talk to you tomorrow." As Murphy hung up the phone he noticed that his hand was shaking. Who was he kidding? Larry was right... he was crazy!

Remembering the doll, Murphy opened the locker: come on, sweetheart, time to go home. Grandpa needs to get you a blanket, wouldn't want you to catch a cold. During the drive back to the compound Murphy talked to the doll that sat next to him on the seat. He was thinking he may as well get used to the child. Little Marie is sure going to be glad to see you, kid, I hope, as he said a silent prayer for his success.

MONDAY

Monday morning: two days and a wake up. Another restless night. A glass of wine tonight might ease the tension. He thought having to follow the rules in the Kingdom was hard, wondering if his grandfather followed the rules during prohibition. Murphy knew his grandfather was connected to Tammany Hall, way back when. Jim Farley had asked him to be a representative in the Bronx borough, but he had declined.

His day would have to end in time to call Chris Brown, perhaps this would be the last call. All he needed was a room number for the hotel, and part of the puzzle would be complete. It dawned on him that he needed a blanket for the doll, yet another stop. Should he check the Yacht Club today or tomorrow? Make it tomorrow, he quickly decided. Murphy wondered if he should call Marie Al Fozi, thinking maybe she could suggest something helpful…any port in a storm.

After breakfast at the compound, Murphy drove to his office. His early arrival assured him of privacy, more time to think. He decided to make a list of things to do. Inspections would be number one, the easy part of the day. Number two, skip lunch and buy a blanket for the baby. Number three was the part that got interesting, call Chris. He had given no thought to a fee, make number four the fee. Change number three, make that, find out the room number. Number four, get Marie's phone number. Talking to Marie could be a mistake, what if she falls apart on me? Let Chris know that he should call her after his call, be sure she is OK. His call to Marie would be number five. That's the plan. Murphy's phone rang at that point.

"Electrical, Murphy."

"When was the last time you had your prostate checked, Michael?"

"Good morning, Larry."

Kelly couldn't help himself. "Do you use your hose every morning, Michael? Have you ever considered a seven-up enema?"

Larry's call did the trick: Murphy was now laughing, "Larry, come on, stop."

"I'm telling you, Michael, you have to keep an eye on everything. The reason I called has to do with your ass, Michael. If something should go wrong, do you have any way to protect yourself?"

Murphy hadn't given that aspect any thought. "Larry, I pray it won't come to that. The bottom line is to protect the child, Larry. If something goes wrong I will give it up, her father gets her back. But first I have to get her away from him, partner, the rest is in God's hands."

Kelly was worried enough for both of them. "I'm going to be in the office this afternoon; wait for me, Michael."

"No problem, Larry, see you later."

Murphy's second inspection was at the office complex. Power had been turned on throughout building three and they were going to check the sub-panels. Lighting panels were 277/480 volt. The same amount of care was taken with lower voltage panels as with higher voltages. One of the workers removed the panel covers and got his tester ready. Each panel had a main breaker that was in the OFF position. Before turning on the main breaker in each panel, all phases were checked to ground, this insures that no dead shorts are present. To test phase-to-ground shorts one sets his tester for continuity with the main breaker off. Testing of all panels went well, no shorts present.

Next would be the test of phases after the main breakers are turned on. You test phase-to-phase and then phase-to-ground in each panel. While Murphy made notes on his check sheets for each panel, the electrician prepared for the voltage test. Murphy stated that he was ready for the phase-to-phase test in the first panel. Noticing that the electrician was having trouble holding the tester and touching the two probes to the phases, Murphy took the tester in his right hand, thinking, three hands can be better than two.

The tester was sitting in the box it came in, facing up so the gauge could be seen. Before Murphy could check the setting on the tester, the electrician put the probes to A and B phases. The tester exploded in Murphy's hand and the box it came in caught fire. Shaking the box free from his hand, Murphy reached for the electrician, to pull him from the front of the panel. The man was visibly shaken but safe. Following protocol, they both had safety glasses on. The electrician had neglected to change the setting of the tester, and Murphy had not picked up on the error in time.

Murphy's second reaction was to check his right hand, still warm but only red, no blisters. "I think you need another tester, partner, if you want to continue."

"Oh yes, Mr. Michael, I will get another one, straight away." came the quick response.

The man had made a mistake but no one was hurt. Murphy, being from the old school, asked the man what he had learned from this incident.

Apologetically, the worker stated, "I am sorry, sir, I was nervous. I didn't tie the panels in, sir, please forgive me, sir."

Murphy smiled and nodded his head. "It's alright, my friend." Many times a worker would be fired for this type of thing but that was not Murphy's style. Had he not known the man and the fact that his work was always good, he may have handled it differently. "Let's have a short break and start again."

"Yes sir, thank you, Mr. Michael." He was so relieved that Murphy took no punitive action. The testing continued after the break and there were no other problems.

Back at the office Murphy dialed Chris Brown's number.

"Brown and Brown." Chris had picked up on the first ring.

"Chris, it's Murphy here."

"Room 363, Michael," Chris immediately confirmed, not wanting to prolong the wait.

"Very good, Chris, you don't fool around, do you?"

Murphy had given quite a bit of thought to the question of what he should charge for his services. "About the fee, Chris, two weeks' pay should cover it."

"And what will that come to?" Chris didn't know how much an electrician was paid over in Saudi Arabia.

"Five thousand; I won't ask for any overtime." Michael considered it a reasonable amount, not putting a premium on the dangerousness of the task. "I have another question for you, Chris, what is Marie's phone number?"

"Are you sure you want to speak to her, Michael?" Marie was a basket-case and Chris was worried that she might upset the apple cart.

Murphy had thought this through, saying, "I'm sure. Wait about an hour and then you call her. If I have any real problem I will call you back right away." At that, Chris gave Murphy the number.

"Okay, Michael, anything else you need?

Murphy made his departure quick, "Got to go, Chris, that's it." Again Murphy hung up before Chris could say anything. Marie's phone rang two times: she must have been sitting next to it, Murphy thought.

A hesitant voice said, "Hello."

"Marie, it's Michael Murphy."

His call evoked concern. "Hello, Mr. Murphy, is something wrong?"

"No, Marie, nothing's wrong. I wanted to make sure you were ready and ask if there was anything else you think I should know. With Chris doing all the middle man stuff there could be something I missed."

"I have my ticket for the round trip, I have a one-way ticket for Marie to the States, and my room number is 363. I don't think I've forgotten anything. I'm so nervous."

Murphy broke in. "Marie, calm down, it's going to be fine. We will see you some time on Friday, afternoon, I think. Whatever you do, Marie, be calm."

"Our tickets back to the States are for Friday, Mr. Murphy. Is that okay?"

"I know, Marie, it's going to be fine." Having said that, Murphy wondered how he was going to handle the passport problem for the child. Worry about that later, he thought, later.

"I have to go, Marie, see you in Bahrain; all's going to be fine."

Larry Kelly walked into Murphy's office as he was hanging up. "What's shaking, brother?"

"Nothing, Larry, just another quiet day in the Kingdom." But Michael was anything but calm.

"Look what I got you, Michael." Kelly held up a small leather case, about the size of two C batteries. "This is just what the doctor ordered."

Murphy took the case and opened it up: a taser. "What am I supposed to do with this?"

Kelly smiled. "I hope you won't need it."

"No kidding, Larry. Where did you get it?" Murphy was busy inspecting the useful weapon.

"The Filipino Mafia, pal." Larry had his connections.

Michael wasn't about to ask any more questions. "Thank you, Larry, but I don't want it."

"You take it, Michael, JIC."

"JIC? What the heck does that mean, Larry?"

"Just in case, pal."

"Okay, now what was it that you wanted me for, Larry?"

"For this, you dummy," Kelly said incredulously.

Feeling somewhat more confident, Murphy stuck the taser into his briefcase and told Larry he had to go. "See you tomorrow, Larry, and thanks again."

TUESDAY

Tuesday morning Murphy found himself more rested than anytime during the last week. Half a bottle of homemade wine had done the trick. Although homemade wine seemed stronger than a good California red, he was rested. He found himself running a little late but that would be no problem today; he was not going to his office. Rather than start at his desk, he had scheduled a start that would permit him to check out the Yacht Club first.

Arriving at the Yacht Club earlier than usual and on a day with no racing scheduled, the guards questioned his reason for being there. "I am here to exercise; I will row for an hour, both today and tomorrow. Big race this weekend, got to be ready."

The guards actually bought it. Although he was all set to pile it on, they simply waved him through. Driving toward the beach area Murphy was, yet again, counting his blessings. There wasn't a soul in sight and the water resembled a mill pond. After taking fifteen minutes to get the inflatable ready and into the water, he was still alone. The trip out was invigorating; I could pull a skier, he thought to himself. As he started down the next to last row out, the paint job on his heart received a huge gouge. The yacht was gone! He forced himself to stand up. Was he in the wrong row? Deep inside he knew: the yacht of choice was gone. One day and a wake up, why now?

A fast glance at the last row showed all six yachts lined up. The one he didn't want to use was sitting there. No engine, no batteries, what else could go wrong? Murphy rowed to the last line of yachts and tied off at his second choice. A check of the shoreline showed that the coast was clear, no pun intended he thought to himself.

Climbing over the side of the yacht Murphy was fighting some terrible thoughts. How could he have gotten himself into this mess? What was he thinking about, how could he give this woman hope, now what? Sliding the hatch cover back he removed the companionway boards. He remembered entering the cabin head first last time; he still had a slight lump on his head to prove it. Look for a battery, check for a GPS… calm down. Once inside he found a GPS but no battery, maybe it's in the cockpit. There was still a set of sails in the bow and the water tanks were still in the same condition, half full. He wondered how long the water had been sitting in those tanks, thinking, what does it matter? Pick up two gallons of water, another stop.

Climbing out of the cabin Murphy secured the hatch boards and slid the cover back in place. He opened the port side seat cover and found fenders and lines, no help. Opening the starboard side Murphy hit pay dirt, two batteries and a master switch. The switch was in the OFF position, a good sign. What the hell, he thought, let's go for it.

Reaching in, he turned the switch to battery one. Above the batteries was an amp meter with a test switch. Pushing the button Murphy expected the worst. The needle jumped, passing the red line and then it flew to the high side of green. Thank you, Lord! Turning the selector switch to battery two, Murphy found himself holding his breath. As he pushed the amp meter button for the second time the reaction was different: slowly the needle climbed past the red line and about midway up the green line it came to a stop. We can do this, he thought, again finding himself thanking his maker. All I need is wind and I'm out of here, Murphy thought.

Once Murphy got the inflatable put away and cleared the Yacht Club property he was feeling better. He was thinking he should pick up a spare battery and a small generator, just to be safe. After he got his inspections behind him he would hit the hardware store. All I need is wind, all I need is wind. Murphy also knew he had to check the Yacht Club tomorrow morning. He knew he couldn't handle another surprise like today, on Thursday morning.

By the time Murphy finished his day he was tired but pleased with his progress. He had picked up everything he felt he needed for backup power. He bought food and water for the passage, all he should need for a round trip. Finishing the second half of his wine bottle, Murphy was ready for another night of complete bed rest. No sooner had he climbed into bed then there was a knock on the door.

As he made his way to the door he stubbed his toe on the spare battery he had purchased. Just what I needed he thought, this better be good. Opening the door and looking into the semi-darkness, Murphy struggled to focus, jumping back when it hit him: Larry Kelly's asshole was looking him straight in the face!

"Larry, you used to be taller."

"Hi, partner," was the only comment.

Murphy, still rubbing his eyes, told him, "I was already in bed, Larry."

"Sorry, Michael, I just wanted to see if you needed any help. Are you ready, Bro?"

"I think I have everything under control, Larry, I sure hope I do. God help me."

The clock was ticking. "You're running out of time, Michael."

"You think I don't know that? I'm ready, Larry. I will need sleep, you know, rest." Murphy was desperately wishing he was in bed already.

"OK, Michael, I'm not going to worry then. You get some sleep and call me if you think of anything I can do." Kelly was anxious for this scheme to get started and be done with.

"Thanks, buddy, for your offer; see you tomorrow then."

WEDNESDAY, THE LAST DAY OF WORK

Once again the wine had done the trick; Murphy was rested. He found himself wishing it was Thursday morning and both he and Kelly were on their way to McDonald's. His schedule for Wednesday was ambitious,. He knew he had to stay busy or he might get nervous. Just when all of this was going through his mind another thought came to him, I sure hope Fozi and family are going to be at McDonald's tomorrow morning. Pretending to slap himself he had his next thought: get ready for work, stupid, now.

Breakfast was light and as always the coffee was nasty. He remembered the time he and Joan had driven to southern New Jersey to visit their daughter at the university. Before they left Joan filled a thermos with coffee for the trip. Upon their arrival at Amanda's school, Michael decided to have a shot of coffee. Amanda picked up on the aroma and asked for a sip. Placing the cup to her lips she took a sip, her eyes closing and her head rolling back as she savored the taste. Coffee from home, she exclaimed, "I forgot how good it is." Michael caught himself anticipating his next cup of coffee made by Joan…it's going to be so good.

Making his way to the office was exciting, as he always enjoyed his last day of work. Considering the fact that he had three near misses due to reckless drivers, he was not going to let anything ruin his day, just another day in the Kingdom. In another five or six hours Marie would be departing for Bahrain and thank God, she would not have to worry about the drivers, not until tomorrow. Peter was at the office and this took Murphy by surprise.

"Good morning, Mr. Michael," came the cheery greeting.

"Good morning, Peter, didn't you go home last night?" Murphy wondered what was up.

Peter began to laugh. "Oh, yes I did, Mr. Michael. Would you like some coffee, sir?"

Murphy smiled, "Funny you should mention coffee, Peter, I was just thinking about a good cup of coffee." Conjuring up Joan's home brewed, Murphy then became reticent.

"I will get you a cup, sir," offered Peter swiftly.

Murphy interrupted Peter, "Thank you, but I think I will pass, Peter. I have to get going straight away."

Peter continued to smile while his head moved from side to side, bobble-head style, "Fine, sir."

Murphy got his paperwork in order and decided which projects he should visit first. If there was going to be any testing today he made a mental note to wear gloves…sailing requires hands that are not burnt.

A final glance at his desk created a new thought, Joan. The picture of his wife: should anything go wrong: how was he going to explain this. Instead of waiting until Sunday and their usual call, he'd better call today. Now he knew he would not let her in on the goings on with him but he thought he better call. Ripping a piece of paper from his sticky pad, he wrote, "Call Joan." Placing the paper dead center of his desk, he departed.

The drive to the Yacht Club went well, out of five intersections he had only had one close call. The guards acted as if he had interrupted their sleep. Waving Murphy in, both guards sat back down and placed their guns against the wall of the guard shack. Making his way to the beach, Murphy had only one thought: please, no surprises. Within fifteen minutes he was in the water and rowing for all he was worth. Before he reached the last row of yachts he had counted the masts, six. Relief or false security, he was not sure, came over him. His next thought, two days from now this will all be behind me. Finally a good thought, as he smiled to himself and started back to the beach.

All inspections went as planned and that put him back at his office about three p.m. As he entered his office area the note he had left on his desk that morning hit him square in the eyes. Maybe she wouldn't be home; if it rings four times he would hang up: the term, chicken shit, crossed his mind. What was going to be his reason for calling today? He knew it had to be good. Ha, he had it: a pump station inspection scheduled for Sunday, in the desert, and he won't be back in time for their regular call.

After dialing the number Murphy was amazed to hear the first ring in mere seconds. Sure, he thought, if this was a regular call it would have taken five minutes, if even he could have gotten through the first time. On the third ring he heard his wife's voice, "Hello."

Murphy couldn't resist, "I just called to say I love you."

Her humor matched his. "I told you never to call me at this number."

Michael continued, "Very funny. Who else might be calling you?"

"What's wrong, Michael? It's not Sunday. "

He never could hide anything from her, but at least she couldn't see the nervous smile on his face. The nervous smile always came over him when he was up to something. She never missed it and would question it every time. "Why does something have to be wrong, Joan?"

"Because I know you too well, Michael Murphy," was her cynical response.

"Alright, you got me. I have to do an inspection in the desert on Sunday. I couldn't change the schedule, I'm sorry."

194

Sarcastically, she went on, "You should do an inspection here once in awhile."

Murphy chose to ignore the tenor of the last comment. "What's up?"

"Well, there's the yard, the leaky faucet in the bathroom, the…"

Murphy had to interrupt his wife, thinking that this was not going to be a good call. "Three weeks, maybe four, I'm home for good, please."

"Right," came Joan's curt reply.

Trying to smooth things over, Michael went on, "As soon as I get back from Sunday's inspection I'll give you a call, is that better?"

Joan wasn't in the mood for much forgiveness. "Sure, call then."

But he persevered, saying, "How are the kids?"

"They're good, they miss you, too. God only knows why." Joan wasn't even trying to cover her annoyance.

"Come on, Joan, give me a break, will you?" Michael didn't want this call to go like this, considering what he was facing.

Joan sounded quite angry when she said, "I could use a break myself, Michael."

Michael knew he was on borrowed time. "Four weeks at the most, I promise."

"At least are you staying out of the sun?" Finally a caring comment came from her lips.

This woman was amazing, Murphy thought. First she breaks my back and in the next breath, shows concern about my skin condition! "I use sun block every day." Thankfully she could not see the nervous smile on his face.

"See that you do." She really did love him, despite his wickedness.

Murphy's phone lit up suddenly, "Let me put you on hold, Joan; I have to take this call."

"Go take care of your business; call me on Sunday."

"Alright, love you; till Sunday."

"Stay safe," were Joan's parting words.

Pushing the button for line two, Murphy announced, "Inspections, Murphy here."

"I got you a hose and some Seven-Up."

Kelly. This was one of the rare times he was happy to hear from his sick buddy. "What's up, now, Larry?"

"Just checking in, Pard, how about dinner in town tonight?"

After giving it quick thought, Murphy thought better of it. "Let's eat in the compound tonight, Larry; I have to get ready, big day tomorrow."

"Okay, Bro, 1800 good?"

"You're on."

"Bye." And with that, Larry was gone.

Murphy hung up and took a deep breath: show time!

A meal with Larry was always an experience, anything could happen. As luck would have it, Kelly went easy on him this night for which he was grateful for the small favor.

Kelly asked, "You ready, Michael?"

Larry didn't have to elaborate; Murphy knew exactly what he was referring to. "Man, I hope so or should I say, 'I'd better be?'"

Another question: "Boat ready?"

Michael was thinking about his trip out to the Yacht Club earlier in the day. "I checked it this morning; it's there."

But Larry kept up the line of questioning. "Think it might be there tomorrow?"

"Buddy, will you please stop? I'm nervous enough without you putting more doubts in my mind." Michael was putting on a good show of confidence, but in his heart and mind…..

"Just kidding, partner, relax. Did I tell you what I have planned for tomorrow, pal?"

Here we go, Murphy thought, "And what is it that you have planned for tomorrow, Larry? I can't wait to find out."

"Well, to start, breakfast with a lady friend at McDonald's."

This made Michael Murphy laugh. Boy, did he need something to break the tension.

"That's better, Michael."

"Okay, Larry, let's end this meal with a smile. Meet me in the morning at 0700; I have a small generator and battery to put in your car, some food and water also."

"It's a date, Bro."

"Will you stop with the term, 'date,' Larry, please."

"OK, Michael, see you in the morning, bright and early."

D DAY

Thursday morning found Michael Murphy rested and ready. The way it was working out seemed simple, one child abduction, a small sailing adventure, and then it was back to the US of A. The prevailing winds would be from the northwest; and with any luck, the dust from Iraq and the Kingdom would be minor. This time of year it was not uncommon for ten to fifteen knot winds with relatively calm seas. After leaving the bay they would head east northeast, similar to the route taken by the King Fahd Causeway which ran from Dhahran to Bahrain. The Gulf of Bahrain to Bahrain itself would measure about thirty miles give or take five miles.

There was a border checkpoint about midway on the causeway and with any luck they would be too far south to be observed. Now the coastal patrols were another matter and they would have to be addressed if the time came. Umm Na'san Island would be the first land that Murphy hoped he would see...it could be all downhill from there.

A sudden rap on the door of Murphy's room nearly brought him out of his skin. Jumping up he knew he was nervous; he had to calm down. Another loud rap caused him to react the same way. He was expecting Kelly and there was no reason for him to announce himself that way. As he opened the door, eyes at normal height, he realized that he had been had again. There was Kelly's ass staring him in the face, pants down, cheeks spread, and the words, good morning, echoing in the background.

Can't you just knock on a door like a normal individual, Larry?"

"I did, Michael."

Murphy thought about what Larry said for a split second and realized that what he did was normal for him. As Larry pulled his pants up and tucked in his shirt he laughed and entered Murphy's room.

"I guess it never occurred to you that I might be a bit uneasy this morning?"

"I'm sorry, Pard."

Murphy closed the door and finally felt at ease. This guy was never going to change and he wondered why he thought he might.

"You ready for breakfast or would you rather wait until we get to McDonald's?" Kelly asked.

"I just want coffee, Larry."

"I can bring the car around, Michael; do you have everything ready?"

"I'm ready and you can have the key. Come back later and take anything you might want. If you don't want anything, let Peter and Paul have the key and they can clean out the place." Murphy grabbed a hanger with his wardrobe for the morning and his heels. Kelly started to laugh.

"Larry, give me a break."

"I can't help it, Michael, I'm sorry."

"Maybe you could grab that cooler and the generator. Did you get me a gallon of gas?"

"I wouldn't let you down, Pard."

"Thanks, now let's get this show on the road."

Before Larry picked anything up he grabbed Michael's arm and looked him straight in the eyes. "You know this is crazy, Michael. If anything goes wrong, I can't help you."

Murphy stood there and was silent for what seemed like an eternity. "You're already helping me, you jerk."

"This part is nothing. I mean if something happens after you get on the boat."

"One thing at a time, Larry; we don't know if the child will want to leave with me."

Still staring at one another Murphy realized his friend of nearly forty years was worried about his welfare, really worried. "This will be over in two days, Larry, but it may be something we won't laugh about in years to come."

Kelly continued to stare at Michael and replied, "I bet we will."

"Come on, Bro, let's go get a Big Mac."

BREAKFAST

Murphy and Kelly sat in front of McDonald's for almost forty-five minutes before the Al Fozie's car pulled into the parking lot. Kelly looked at Murphy, who had changed into his disguise and remarked, "By God, you did it, Brother, look at this."

As they watched the family get out of the car you could hear a pin drop: first Fozi, then the woman, and when Fozi opened the back door of the Chevy Caprice, the children. Little Marie resembled Shirley Temple and the boy was packing a video game which he never stopped playing from the time he slid out of the car to the trek across the parking lot. Once they entered the building and the door closed behind them Murphy decided to give them time to get to the family area and get their order in. Checking his watch he decided that fifteen minutes would be enough time for them to be seated and served.

On the seat between Kelly and Murphy was the portable DVD player and more important, the Rag Doll the child loved so much. It was at this time that Murphy realized how hard it was to see through the black material which the abia was made of. Watching the family outside in the sun was not hard but everything changed when you were under a cover such as the roof of the car. All he could hope for was that the lighting in McDonald's was bright enough to permit good vision; after all, Arab women had no problems, did they. Five minutes passed and again, it seemed like an hour had gone by. Murphy's feet were already sore from the shoes; they seemed tight and a size or two, too small.

"When we go in, do you want to sit near the family while I get the coffee, Michael?"

"That's a good idea, Larry, do that."

"How do you like your coffee, Michael?"

"What?"

"How do you like your coffee?"

Murphy's head turned towards Kelly with a questioning look on his face.

"Well, do you want sugar?"

"Alright, I will take sugar."

"How about cream?"

Again Murphy's head turned to Kelly.

"Cream?"

"Yes, cream. I'll take cream."

"How many creams?"

Murphy turned to Kelly again.

"Will you knock it off, Larry; can't you see I have a lot on my mind?"

"Not with that thing over your head, I can't see you at all."

"I'm sorry if I seem jumpy, Larry."

"No problem, Michael."

"One sugar or two?"

Murphy turned to Kelly, yet again, "That's it, make it black, no sugar."

"You don't have to get huffy about it, Brother."

Looking down at his watch Murphy could see that all the useless banter with Larry had eaten up another five minutes. Larry reached for the door handle and opened it, "I have to take a leak."

"And you're going to do it there?"

"Why not, it's a perfectly normal body function."

"I really need to get popped for this, Larry; can't you wait until we go inside?"

"OK, but you know it's not healthy to hold it."

Looking down at his watch Murphy stated that they were going in, in three minutes.

Before they knew it the time had come. Murphy grabbed his props and they started for the door.

SHOW TIME

L arry Kelly purposely walked fast in order to arrive at the front door of the restaurant ahead of Murphy. As he opened the door he motioned for his lady friend to enter. "Always the gentleman," Murphy said. The restaurant was not busy and they walked directly into the family section. At a glance Murphy counted six tables occupied. The Al Fozie family was located near the amusement section and as far away from the rest rooms as they could be.

Larry saw to it that Michael was seated before he went to the counter to order. Fozi and his wife were eating, the children watched the sliding board as other kids took their turns on the ride. Fozi's son watched the ride and played with the video game at the same time while little Marie just stared. One of the rides was a giant corkscrew kind of configuration that a child would have to climb to a height of ten feet to slide down. The climb was protected by a tunnel type ladder that would permit an adult to accompany their child. The more Murphy looked at the situation the more he thought that the corkscrew was the place to make contact.

Larry got back to the table with Murphy's coffee and a fist full of something he planned to eat.

"Turkey bacon!" Larry gasped.

From under the black veil came the words, "Turkey what?"

"Turkey bacon, that's all they have here and get this, they want to know how many feces."

"How does it look for getting a chance to talk to the little girl, Michael?"

"Not sure yet, but once she's finished with her breakfast it won't take long to figure out."

"Have you figured out how you're going to drink that coffee, Michael?"

"Not yet my friend."

"You don't look bad in that veil; hey, how about I get you a straw?"

Before Michael could answer Kelly, Marie got up and headed for the sliding board. Murphy noticed that as long as Fozi and his wife had been sitting at the table, not a word had been spoken, and the young man, still played on the video game. Marie climbed up the small sliding board and for the first time Murphy saw the child smile. While the Al Fozies had not spoken, they had not paid much attention to the children, either.

This has to be it, Murphy thought. I have to get up and be ready for the next time Marie approaches the ladder. As he rose from the seat he felt pressure on his shoulders and heard the distinct sound of material tearing. It didn't take him long to figure out that he had just put a heel through his aba. Lowering himself back down on his chair he began to adjust the new problem. Kelly was attempting to not laugh and that didn't help matters any. On his return trip to the chair when he also dropped the doll, he could feel sweat on his forehead; what next?

"You gonna make it, Brother?"

"I don't know man, here goes."

His second attempt went well; he was up and still had the doll and DVD player in hand. He looked toward the small slide and found that Marie was no longer there. She had returned to the table while he was fussing with his wardrobe. Now what? No sooner than he sat back down, Marie was up and this time headed for the corkscrew slide, alone. Murphy was up and again there were no mishaps. Marie was on her way up the long ladder before he could get close. A glance toward the table showed no attention had been paid to the little girls' actions. Would she do this slide twice - was the sixty-four dollar question.

Standing at the foot of the ladder Murphy watched as another child, accompanied by her mother, started for the top. Marie had started her descent and Murphy could hear the child giggle and laugh as she reached the opening at the floor.

Murphy realized that he was soaking wet from sweat. Thankfully he did not detect any shaking. He checked the table to see if Fozi was still sitting with his wife; he was. This was it, he had to move now. Another child passed Murphy as he stood at the foot of the ladder and Marie was walking directly toward him. Murphy watched as she quickly moved past him and started up the ladder. Once the little girl was up to the fifth rung he did it, he called to her.

"Is this your doll, Marie?"

The child stopped climbing and looked back. At first there was no reaction, only a long look. Again Murphy asked the question, "Is this your doll, Marie?"

While the child was looking at the doll, Murphy could see a smile forming on her face.

"Yes, that's my Annie! Where did you get her, how do you know my name?"

Murphy reached for the child, lowered her down to the floor and handed her the doll.

"My name is Michael Murphy and your mother sent me here to get you, if you want to go home to her. She sent your doll and I have this. He pulled the DVD out from under his aba and opened it. Michael moved the child out of the way of the line of mothers and children behind them.

"We have to hurry, Marie, watch this." It only took two minutes for the child to watch enough to know she wanted to see her Mom.

"You can't say anything to your dad; this has to be a secret, Marie."

"How come you're dressed like that, Michael Murphy?"

"It's a long story, Marie."

"Where is my mommy, when can I see her?"

"You have to come with me on a short trip, and we should be with her tomorrow."

At this point Murphy noticed that Fozi was looking in their direction.

"Remember this is a secret, Marie, you can't tell your dad. Go back to the table and when I wave to you, we are on our way."

The little girl continued to smile and hug the rag doll.

"OK, Michael Murphy, when you wave we will be on our way."

The child started back to the table and Murphy realized that she was still hugging the doll. As quietly as possible he called to the little girl, "Marie, Marie."

Spinning around and still smiling, she stopped.

Murphy motioned for her to come back. "I better keep Annie with me, Marie, you know, it's a secret."

Marie handed the doll to Murphy and again he repeated the word, "secret."

The little girl ran off and she was still smiling. As for Murphy, he was sweating like crazy and a shake had developed. Upon returning to his table he found his legs to be a bit rubbery.

"What happened?" Larry asked.

"She wants to go with us, Larry."

"When?"

"Soon, Larry."

Murphy watched the child take her seat at her table. For some reason she began to speak to Mrs. Al Fozie. Her father had gotten involved with reading a paper and her brother was still hitting the buttons on the video player.

THE SURPRISE

Murphy sat quietly staring through the black material that hid him from the rest of the world. His mind was doing a hundred miles an hour and he still could not believe this little child trusted him enough to go with him.

"Larry, go outside and give our friend a flat tire, will you."

"Just one, Michael?"

"Just one and then start your car and be ready."

"Want me to take your coffee with me?"

"Just go, Larry, please."

Once Larry was out of the building Murphy went back to staring through the veil at the Al Fozie family. Little Marie was doing something that resembled whispering to Fozi's wife and then the woman would whisper in Marie's ear. Fozi continued to read the paper while the boy continued to play with the video game.

Suddenly the little fellow put the video game down on the table and said something to Fozi. He didn't seem to hear the boy and continued to read. The boy jumped up and went around the table to his father where he now pulled at Fozi's arm. Murphy could not hear what was going on but he knew, or felt, something was up. Fozi pushed the paper back on the table and stood up. Taking the boy's hand, they started toward the rest rooms.

This was it. Murphy motioned to the child, pointed to the slide and got up. He could not believe what he saw next... both Marie and the woman got up and moved in his direction. When the woman and the child got to Murphy he was not ready for what he was about to hear. The woman leaned in close and said, "You have to take me, too."

Without thinking, Murphy took Marie's hand and all he could think to say was, "Let's go!" The three of them walked as fast as they could without running, clearing the front door in seconds. Kelly had done what he was told and not only did he start the car, he had moved it to the front of the building. The door on the passenger side flew open and all Murphy could see was a very puzzled look on the driver's face.

"What the hell is going on?"

Murphy pushed the child in as gently as possible, next he climbed in, his last move was to pull the woman in on his lap. Slamming the door he motioned to Larry and they were off.

"What's going on, Michael?"

"Just drive, Larry, I'm not sure myself"

After clearing the parking lot Kelly headed the car southbound.

"Did you take care of that little problem for me?"

"I did, Michael."

"This was going to be our little secret, Marie. What happened?"

Then came Murphy's next shock. The woman on his lap pulled her veil back. She was not Saudi; she appeared to be of Philippine descent.

"I want to go to the Philippine Embassy, please."

"I can't take you to the embassy here; you don't understand, we are leaving the country."

"You have to take me with you, anywhere."

Murphy knew that most of the servants in the Kingdom were from the Philippines and in some cases, they were not happy with the positions they ended up in. His plan was going to be hard enough with just a child. How was he going to pull this off? If he dropped her off somewhere she might report him. He needed some time to think and there was none. He would have to take her with them. Hell, they were already on their way to the boat.

Larry had not said a word to this point and Michael knew he was going to hear something soon. By now Fozi had to know his daughter and servant were gone. What Murphy didn't know was that once Fozi and his son returned from the rest room they would sit down at their table and resume what they had been doing. Fifteen minutes would pass before Fozi looked for his daughter and servant.

Once Kelly cleared Dhahran he pulled the car over. Murphy thought, here it comes.

"What's the plan, Michael?"

"Before we get to the marina let's pull over and rearrange the car. We can put the girls in the back on the floor, cover them with our gear, and pile it high. I know these guys and they know me. Just get back on the road, Larry; you drive, I'll think."

REPACKING THE CAR

Kelly headed south as directed and refrained from asking any more questions. Murphy knew there were not many places to stop along the way; the beach road was not like at home. In the good old USA there would be one store after another selling all sorts of water sports fun equipment. Then it hit him, there was a large building that was shaped like a giant hotdog on a bun just before the Sunset Cove turn off. He could not remember the name of the hotdog stand but it would be a place they could pull into and do what needed to be done.

"Larry, when we get to that hotdog stand near Sunset Cove let's stop there."

"OK, Michael."

"Pull as far off the road as you can."

"Alright, Bro."

"They may not be open but what else can go wrong?"

Murphy pulled the rag doll out from under his costume and handed it to Marie. Between the DVD player and the woman sitting on his lap he was very uncomfortable. Before long the hotdog stand came into view so there was no reason to complain now. Larry eased the car into the parking lot and drove as far to the rear as he could go; there was one car in front of the place and two pickups in back.

"OK, everybody out." Helping the woman out, he was still not sure how she would react.

"What's your name, young lady?"

"My name is Sophia."

"Do you understand what is going on here?"

"Yes I do."

"I can't say for sure that we will make it, but our goal is Bahrain."

"I can go to the embassy there and I will be safe."

Murphy kicked off the heels that were killing him at this point; next came the shedding of his aba. Marie climbed out of the car and looked him straight in the eyes. "When are we going to be there, Mr. Murphy?"

Now there was a phrase Murphy had not heard in many years: when are we going to be there. "We are going to take a short trip on a sailboat, Marie, and by tomorrow, maybe in time for lunch, you should be with your mom."

"What about my dad?"

"I don't think he will be there, Marie, just your mom."

"What about my brother?"

"I don't think he will be there either." Murphy bent down on his knees and reached out to pull the little girl up close.

"Marie, are you sure you want to do this? I can get you back to your father if you want."

"I want to be with my mom, I'm sure."

Murphy stood up and now turned to Sophia. "Are you sure you want to do this? If anything goes wrong we are going to be in some serious trouble."

"I'm sure."

Murphy opened the back door of the car and started to empty out the stuff onto the parking lot. "Larry, why don't you and Sophia check out the stand. If it's open, I still could use a coffee, black no sugar. See what Marie wants and she can stay here with me while I get the car ready. No one would think it unusual to see Larry with a woman who was covered but he didn't want the child to be seen.

Larry and Sophia were gone for almost fifteen minutes and Murphy was beginning to be concerned. Suddenly they appeared and they had a tray full of goodies.

"Lets take a break everybody, fifteen minutes, and then we can repack the car." After the break Murphy explained what had to be done. Since they were only about five minutes from the Sunset Cove turnoff, he knew the woman and the child could handle being on the floor with some supplies piled on top of them. Sophia got into the back seat and lowered herself onto the floor.

"Get on your knees and try to roll yourself up in a ball, Sophia." Somehow she managed to take up only the area behind Kelly's seat. Next Murphy helped Marie in; she would occupy the floor behind Murphy's seat. "This is fun, Mr. Murphy."

"Marie, once we're finished packing the car you can't talk anymore; it's like we are playing hide and seek."

"OK, Mr. Murphy."

"Are you alright, Sophia?"

"I am."

Murphy closed both back doors and started to pile sleeping bags and beach chairs on top of his passengers. The cooler he placed on the back seat and then there were two blankets next to that. Now he opened the doors to see if the girls could be seen on the floor. No problem.

"This is it ladies, are you ready?"

The good thing was that he could hardly hear their reply.

"No more talking until I say it is clear." Murphy climbed into the front seat and looked at Kelly.

"Let's do it, Larry."

THE FINAL GATE

Approaching the main gate of Sunset Cove the two men found themselves in a line of cars and pickups. Just to add to the pressure of clearing the gate they would have to wait for five or six vehicles ahead of them. Murphy hoped that no one would piss off the guards before they got their turn to be checked. The sun was getting rather high in the sky and Murphy could feel the temperature rising in the car.

"You better put the air on low and shut the windows, Larry."

Larry didn't respond to Michael's request.

"Larry, did you hear me?"

"Hear you."

"Are you OK, Larry?"

"Yeah, Bro, I'm OK."

"Would you put the air on low and crank up you window?"

"Yeah, I heard you."

"You're nervous, aren't you?"

"I'm fine."

Murphy leaned over to Larry and whispered, "Horseshit."

"You're right, I feel like a whore in church."

"Don't fail me now, Brother."

"I'll be fine, just let's clear this gate."

Kelly edged forward until his turn came. Rolling down both windows they could see that one of the guards was going back to the shack. The remaining guard approached the driver side and made the customary gesture for their IDs. Larry presented his papers and the guard did his usual scan. Murphy wondered if they ever really checked what was in their hand.

When the guard motioned to Murphy for his papers he reached across Larry's steering wheel. For some reason Murphy started to hand the papers with his left hand. The guard pulled back his hand and frowned; Murphy immediately pulled back his hand and put the papers in his right hand. The guard half smiled and once again reached for Murphy's papers. Murphy apologized for the disrespect. Murphy always wondered if they knew which hand a right hander from New York wipes his ass with.

After handing back Murphy's papers the guard motioned to Kelly to open the back door locks. When Kelly did as he was told, the guard opened the rear door. Murphy opened his door and got out of the car. Rounding the back of the car, he asked the guard if he wanted him to empty the car out. Shaking his head no, the guard reached into the car and lifted the top blanket which sat next to the cooler. Murphy felt as if it was just a matter of time before they were all going to jail, it was over. The guard picked up the second blanket and now there was nothing between Sophia and a sleeping bag. Dropping the blankets back onto the sleeping bag the guard started for the passenger side of the car, Murphy followed. Opening the remaining rear door the guard asked what was in the cooler, wine maybe?

"No sir, lunch," Murphy replied. He reached into the car and opened the cooler top. Using his right hand Murphy produced a can of Pepsi and offered it to the guard. Shaking his head no, the guard refused the can of soda. With that, Murphy placed the can back in the cooler and closed the top.

Next the guard motioned to have the trunk opened. Murphy wondered what the guard would think when he saw the generator and the small gas can. Kelly popped the trunk lid as the guard walked to the back of the car. As the guard reached for the lid the car behind them honked his horn three times. As the guard opened the trunk lid he turned toward the car behind him, raised his hand and yelled, shway, shway.. He was telling the driver to calm down. The driver honked once again and now the guard was getting annoyed. Turning back to the open trunk the guard closed the lid and motioned to Kelly to move through. Murphy walked to the passenger side and got in. It was over.

Once inside the gate they went to a spot where two cars had parked and left a space in between them.

"OK, ladies, we made it."

No one saw the woman and the girl get out of the car, and as far as Murphy was concerned they were in the clear. Murphy told Kelly to put the trunk contents in front of the car and then hang out for a little while. If he left straight away the guards might pick up on the fact that the car was empty and he was now alone.

Kelly handed Murphy an envelope.

"What's this, Pard?"

"Your passport and some money."

"You're the best, Larry."

BAHRAIN BOUND

Spending the day at Sunset Cove was a nice change but what Murphy really wanted to do was row out to the outside line of yachts. The sooner they could get out there the sooner they could leave. Marie spent the day playing on the beach while Sophia watched her. Murphy went to the lost-and-found where he got each of them a bathing suit. Sophia as it turned out was in her mid twenty's, all of five feet tall, and nearly one hundred pounds. In three years she had never been to the beach. This was hard since she grew up just a stone's throw from the beach in her homeland.

Kelly had taken off after spending two hours with Murphy and the girls. Marie and Kelly hit it off because he helped her build a huge sand castle. Murphy figured it was Sophia that really kept Kelly around. He was more than twice her age but his mind was always working. He had been gone for at least an hour, so Murphy felt there was nothing to worry about; he had to have had no trouble clearing out of the gate.

Most of the beach people had left by five o'clock so Murphy decided to grab a launch from the tender storage area. Rather than use his friend's tender he would pick one he could leave adrift and not be connected to.

Murphy dragged the tender down to the beach and loaded it with everything he had. He didn't want to make two trips out to the yacht but with the girls he thought the gunnels may go under water. He called to Sophia and Marie; this would be the test. He got in and manned the oars. First Sophia placed Marie in the bow of the tender and then she slowly climbed into the stern. This was going to be close, and thank God there were no large waves. No one seemed to pay attention to the little tender as it worked its way out to the waiting yacht.

By the time they reached the outside row and the third little yacht in, Murphy had had enough. A glance toward shore proved to be fruitful, nobody watching and nobody near the tender storage area. First Murphy lifted Marie into the boat, next Sophia climbed in. Once he had handed them all the supplies, he tied the tender off and boarded himself.

Getting everything put away didn't take long and the girls liked the cabin below. Murphy would wait until dark to put the sails on; doing it in daylight would surely get them noticed. He checked and rechecked the running rigging in order to prevent a problem after dark. Batteries were still showing some life and he bumped the cabin lights, still good. Now he knew they would not be using running lights or cabin lights but they needed power for the engine. Murphy had a flash light with him that cast a red light; red is for night vision.

Most of the food Murphy had packed was snack type stuff. Neither Marie nor Sophia complained about that since he had fed them a hot meal at the marina restaurant an hour or so before leaving shore. He could not get over how well the woman and the child got along. All the times he had observed them he couldn't remember ever seeing them smile. When he asked Sophia about his observation she merely told him that there was never much to smile about. Marie asked him if he would teach her to sail; again he flashed back - he'd taught three kids to sail, his kids. Marie wanted to know if her mom could sail with us. "Maybe when we get back to New York, sports model." She wanted to know why he called her sports model. "Your size, young lady."

The hour was 5:42 p.m.; we shall head out at 9:00 p.m. The girls found their way down to the cabin by six o'clock and both of them had sacked out. Murphy didn't want them awake during the night if he could help it, so he asked them if they wanted to play cards.

"I can play 'go fish,' Marie said."

Sophia said she also knew how to play 'go fish.'

"Well then, 'go fish' it is." Seems as if that is a perfect game for three people on a sailboat.

For the next two and a half hours, the three sailors laughed, drank soda and munched on potato chips, and forgot how much trouble they could be in.

ANCHORS AWAY

By eight-thirty Murphy had been beaten at 'go fish' more times than he cared to admit. He now knew Sophia was very intelligent and for the first time in a very long time, happy. For the life of him he was not sure of what he was going to do with her. The Philippine Embassy in Bahrain was near Marie Al Fozie's hotel and that was their only hope. The child on the other hand was another story. Not being able to contact Larry for any feedback on the situation in town played on his mind.

Murphy knew it was time to get the show on the road.

"You guys hang in while I get the boat ready. Give me about fifteen minutes and I will need you on deck."

It didn't take long to get the pennants prepared and he was calling down to Sophia. This would be her first test; she would have to take the wheel while he cut the boat loose from the mooring.

After explaining to Sophia that she would gently turn the boat wheel to starboard when he yelled clear, the fun began. Sophia wanted to know which way was starboard and this caused Murphy to laugh. This is going to be fun, he thought.

"I'm sorry Sophia; turn the wheel gently to the right. Do you know how to drive Sophia?

"Yes, Mr. Murphy, I know how to drive. My dad taught me when I was seventeen."

"Great," Murphy replied.

"I haven't been behind a wheel in three years, Mr. Murphy, but I remember."

"Well, let's do it, young lady."

Murphy went forward and untied the first pennate, he then tied it to the tender. Looking back he could see Sophia waiting behind the wheel and ready. He uncleated the second pennate and tossed it into the tender. Looking back again, he yelled 'clear' to Sophia and they began to fall off to the right. It should have taken Murphy only a few seconds to get back to the wheel and take over but he moved slowly. He figured that he should let her get the feel of the wheel and show her that he was confident in her.

The little boat drifted off the mooring to the right and the wind headed them in the correct direction. Murphy decided to leave Sophia at the wheel while he raised the main sail. Standing next to the new sailor, he then instructed her to come to a compass heading of 90 degrees. He showed her where that was and then instructed her to find a star that she could aim at. The young lady did everything he told her. She might be a natural, he thought. Murphy climbed up onto the cabin top and grabbed the halyard on the right side of the mast. As he raised the main sail he could feel the boat accelerate.

"Concentrate on the star, kid, don't be nervous."

"Something happened to the wheel, Mr. Murphy, it feels different."

Remaining on the cabin top Murphy simple instructed the girl to concentrate on her star and the boat continued to accelerate.

"You're doing great kid, hold your course."

"My course?"

"Just follow your star," Murphy replied.

Murphy knew it was about four miles to the Gulf of Bahrain and that would take about thirty minutes. Darkness was surrounding them now that they were away from the yacht club. Darkness was good. Murphy moved back to the cockpit and stood next to his sailing student. Little Marie was standing in the companionway looking out with her rag doll under one arm. So far so good.

"Mr. Murphy, I have to go to the bathroom." So much for so far so good, Murphy thought.

Murphy went below as soon as he asked Sophia if she was alright for a minute or so.

Opening the door to the head, Murphy asked the little girl if she could read. It only took a second to realize he had made a big mistake.

"Mr. Murphy, I'm eight years old. I've been reading for years and who beat you at 'go fish'?"

Murphy put his hands up in front of his face and pulled back, "I'm sorry, I'm sorry."

Until now Murphy had only turned on the compass light, which was red. Now what? He handed the little girl his red flashlight and told her to follow the directions next to the seat.

"Aren't you going to tell me to make sure I don't loose your flashlight?"

Murphy could only smile after the child's question. "You want me to hold Annie while you're in there?"

"I don't know, Mr. Murphy; you won't forget where you put her, will you?"

Murphy smiled again, "I'll be very careful, Marie."

Upon returning to the cockpit Murphy scanned the area around the boat and things still were clear. Sophia was still heading toward her star and the compass was right on 90 degrees. Time passed and again Murphy began to feel a false security. That was to end post haste. Suddenly, off to the right and out about a mile, Murphy saw a red light moving across their bow. Jumping onto the cabin top once again Murphy grabbed the main halyard and released it. The main sail fell to the boom.

"Keep following your star Sophia, hold your course."

"What's wrong, Mr. Murphy?"

"There's a boat near the mouth of the bay. I don't know what it is and I don't want him to see us."

No sooner than Murphy said that there were suddenly two lights, a green had joined the red. What ever it was it had just turned into Sunset Cove and was headed straight at them. Murphy knew it was just a matter of seconds before whatever it was would be on top of them. Michael Murphy got the same feeling he had at the gate only hours ago: it's over.

As quickly as the green light appeared, the red light disappeared. They changed course, they were heading away from them, veering to the left. As the power boat passed them, there could not have been more than one hundred yards between them. They had dodged another bullet.

During the time that all this had taken place the little yacht had nearly lost its hull speed completely. As the power boat disappeared into the west Murphy went forward and raised the main sail again. They were closing on the Gulf of Bahrain and soon it would be time to put up the head sail.

"Hold your course kid, you're doing great." Murphy noticed that Sophia was now responding to the term, hold your course.

226

"Mr. Murphy, where's Annie?"

Nuts, what had he done with the doll? This could be serious.

"Look by the table little one, near the cards."

"I found her."

"Mr. Murphy, could I watch the DVD of mommy again?"

"Sure, there may be some Little House on the Prairie DVD's in there, too, Marie."

"I just want to see mommy."

Murphy was getting ready to put the head sail up. He knew that it would be time for him to take the wheel after the head sail was up. They would be clearing Ra's al Khaththaq point and from there on they would be in the Gulf of Bahrain. The little yacht was moving through the water at about four knots and this would get them to Bahrain by sunup.

A scan of the water showed no movement around them and the power boat that had passed by them was now a memory. Murphy took the wheel from Sophia and told her to go below and get some rest, keep an eye on Marie. Maybe five or six hours and this would all be over.

ONE THIRD DOWN

About 2230 hours (10:30 p.m.) Murphy checked his watch for the tenth time; the sky was clear, the Gulf was rather flat, and the winds were nine to twelve knots and steady. The little yacht was on a broad reach and Murphy was watching for signs of the King Fahd Causeway. Considering the fact that they were making about four knots and were on a compass course of zero-eight-five degrees they may have only four or five hours to go. The girls were both below and he had not heard a sound in some time. Sleep would do them good. With any luck they could be past or at least to the territorial waters, the imaginary line between Saudi Arabia and Bahrain.

Now and then a passenger plane would appear; at this point they looked to be in a pattern for the airport at Al Muharraq in Bahrain. Around 2330 (11:30 p.m.) a light plane flew over them and he appeared to be only four or five hundred feet up. Murphy watched it closely and when it turned around he did another of his speed runs to the mast and this time he released both halyards. The sails came sliding down and the main was all over the cabin top, a mess. The plane seemed to drop in altitude as it neared them but again, no sign of being spotted. Murphy called down to Sophia for help with the wheel but there was no answer. Again he called down and this time she responded. Soon she was standing in the companionway rubbing her eyes.

"Are we there yet?"

"Not yet, but I need you to steer again, Sophia."

"Alright, Mr. Murphy, I'm coming."

Sophia took the wheel and waited for Murphy to hoist the sails. Somehow she got the boat on the course he had told her to find. A quick glance around caused Murphy's old heart to skip a beat; the causeway had come into view. Now all they had to do was hold a course parallel to the causeway and watch for Umm Na'san Island. When the island came into view they would keep it to port and head due east.

Murphy sent the young girl below. Having her along had turned out to be a godsend. It was now well after twelve o'clock and he knew they were beyond Saudi waters.

Checking his watch again he saw that it was now past one o'clock. From the east he noticed a boat proceeding in their direction; now what? The boat looked to be very large and no more than three miles away; he could be wrong since it was dark. He would hold his course for a little longer; he didn't want to go through the sail drop again. He soon realized that the boat was not closing on them, they were closing on it. Could it be a fishing boat, perhaps a party boat? After all it had been coming from the direction of Bahrain.

Murphy did a jibe in order to give the craft plenty of room to their port. As close as he could figure they had to be less than a mile south of the boat when they passed it. In about fifteen minutes Murphy decided to jibe again and get back on course. The craft was still in sight of the little sailboat. For our next crisis, a search light came on and began to rotate around the large power boat. As it came around to them the sailboat lit up like a Christmas tree; there was no time to dump the sails. At this time all Murphy could do was hold his course, he did one more thing, he saluted the vessel. Continuing on he waited for the craft to start in his direction but it never did. Why were they using a search light, why did they hold it on them, why didn't they approach? Wiping his forehead with his shaking hand, he just held his course.

Now it was three o'clock and he could barely see the causeway off to the port side. He was tired, very tired. He hadn't seen any more boats since the search light incident, only the occasional passenger plane on its approach. Looking over the bow Murphy thought he saw something ahead, could it be? Bigger than shit, there it was, Umm Na'san Island. Fall off, Michael, fall off, keep it to port. The girls were probably sound asleep and all he wanted to do was wake them up; we might make it gang. Murphy fell off and let the sails out some. Another hour or so, maybe two.

Once Murphy had the island dead to port he could see the lights of Bahrain, beautiful Bahrain. The last time he felt this way he had just spotted Bermuda after twelve days at sea alone. Since he had no idea of what the shoreline held in store for him, he decided to relax. Who was he kidding?

LAND HO

Pushing on past Umm Na'san Island Murphy noticed that the breeze seemed to increase. The northwest wind was up to twenty knots as close as he could figure, and there seemed to be gusts to twenty-five or more. Their little yacht was now cutting through the waves at about seven knots and Murphy started thinking about reducing sails. The worst part about reducing sails is that when you think it time to do it, it's usually too late. Sophia would have to take the wheel if he was going to reduce anything safely. This should be fun.

Murphy called down to Sophia and, thank God, she came right up. After explaining to her what he was going to do, she once again took the wheel. Finding some line to use for reefing, Murphy went up on deck. The process is usually not exciting unless it is at night and you are in high winds. For Murphy it was just another night. One thing, he could not chance using a flashlight, not here, not tonight. There was a good amount of dust in the air; it blows in from Iraq and Saudi Arabia.

Sophia was getting nervous and kept asking if it was alright for the side of the boat to be under water. That happened on the gusts. "Hold your course, Sophia, find a light on shore and head for it, as if it were a star." The young girl was becoming overwhelmed; things had to be done soon. Murphy threaded the line through the sail and tied one end to the forward end of the boom. Next he released the main halyard to let it down, no good. Securing the halyard again, Murphy went back to the nervous girl.

"When I yell to you, turn the boat into the wind. When you feel the wind coming straight at you, turn the wheel gently back to the right. OK?"

"I'll try, Mr. Murphy."

"You can do it, ready?"

Moving back to the mast Michael Murphy released the main halyard once again. Calling out to Sophia he waited as the bow of the boat started around. He knew this had to be fast. He released all pressure on the halyard and cinched up the reef line. Holding the line with his left hand he reached and pulled on the halyard with his right hand and ran it around the cleat. The bow of the boat fell off to starboard as Murphy secured the reefing line. They had done it.

The boat was more stable now and the rail was no longer in the water. His next move would be to let the head sail down; he would not bother Sophia about this move. "Hold your course kid, I'm proud of you." As he reached for the jib halyard a gust caught the little boat, Murphy was thrown forward and off the boat. He would never be able to explain what went through his mind at that moment: a sailor's greatest fear, to be thrown from his vessel. The time he spent moving through the air seemed endless. When would he feel the water, what about the kids?

Murphy heard Sophia scream and suddenly he landed against something hard and it absorbed his whole body. He had been thrown off the boat deck and onto the headsail. The boat was over, the rail was down, Murphy was on the sail. As the boat recovered the mast began to come up. Murphy found himself sliding down the sail and he ended up being deposited on the foredeck. Grabbing the rail Murphy found it hard to move; what had just happened, what had just happened to him, this was the stuff you read about in books. Sophia yelled to Murphy and it brought him around. He felt like this had all been a dream, a good one though.

"I'm OK, kid, I'm OK."

On his second attempt to release the jib halyard he was successful. They were now under control. When he got back to Sophia she was crying. He took the wheel with his left arm, and he hugged her with his right arm.

"Young lady, was that exciting or what?"

Out of the companionway came the voice of Marie, "What's going on, are we there yet?"

Looking at one another they both started laughing.

COAST HOTEL, BAHRAIN

Four a.m., Friday morning, Coast Hotel, room 363. Marie Al Fozie sat staring at the phone next to her bed. She wasn't sure if she had been doing the same thing for two or three days now. The flight to Bahrain had been long and very noisy; there was a child who cried from Heathrow Airport to within thirty minutes before touchdown in Bahrain. A few people had complained but the child's mother could do nothing to stop her. One fellow went so far as to yell from the front of the plane, can't you shut that kid up back there. In response the mother yelled back, if you think you can do better, you try.

Marie knew that her daughter was en route while she was sitting there but there would be no word until Murphy reached Bahrain. Marie Al Fozie had no idea that her child was sailing to Bahrain; as far as she knew they would drive across the causeway like everyone else did. Since leaving the United States there had been no contact with Chris Brown and she had thought about checking in with him. She decided that if she had no word from Murphy by eleven o'clock that morning she would call the Browns. On second thought, what could they do?

Chris Brown closed a file on the case he would be involved with in the morning. He had spent most of his day thinking about what could be going on eight thousand miles from him. He even thought about calling Michael Murphy's house to find out if his wife had heard anything from him in the last day or so. But then again, he didn't want to alarm Murphy's wife for any reason... would Murphy have mentioned to her what he was there for... forget the call.

Jane Brown walked into the room and caught Chris stating into space. "A penny for your thoughts, Chris."

"This case tomorrow has been nothing but problems, love," Chris replied.

"Chris, it's me, what's really wrong?"

For as long as he could remember he had not spoken of what was going on with Marie Al Fozie. He knew Jane was not happy about the whole thing. Now he was wondering if he should tell her that Murphy may have the child and be on his way to Bahrain. One thing for sure, he had better say something.

"It's Marie, right?"

Chris looked into his wife's eyes and told her the truth, "Yes Jane, it's all going down as we speak, I think. I've had no word from Murphy but the plan was to have Marie's daughter in Bahrain before we get up tomorrow morning. "

Jane shook he head and smiled, "It's almost over?"

Chris didn't smile; he simply nodded his head, yes.

Four-thirty and still no word, Marie was not sure how much of this quiet she could stand. She tried to convince herself that things were going to be fine, just a few more hours, maybe two, maybe four, by eleven for sure.

LANDFALL

Umm Na'san Island was barely visible to stern while the lights of Bahrain grew clearer and clearer. Thirty-five minutes had passed since all the excitement; with the sails reduced in size, they enjoyed the rest. Murphy was thinking about running the engine for a short time; the compass light was the only draw on the batteries to this point. They may need power out of a situation in the near future and he didn't want any surprises. Murphy went below and turned the battery switch to both. He also got the ignition key.

Sophia was getting better with the wheel, and again Murphy wondered what he would have done without her. Marie watched the DVD below and played with Annie, still having Murphy's flashlight to see by. The sun would be rising soon so rather than deprive the child of the light, he just let her be.

The eastern sky began to brighten and the skyline of Bahrain gave the crew of the little yacht hope. Murphy estimated an hour and they would make landfall, maybe less. Once the shoreline was clearly in view, he had to decide whether a dock situation was safe or just run the boat aground. Once on shore he had to contact Marie Al Fozie. He wanted to get the child to her mother as soon as possible. Finding a phone may take some time but if that were the biggest problem they had, that would be fine.

Sophia held her course; she had been aimed at a water tower for the last hour. Again Murphy spotted bow lights in the distance and they were coming straight at them. Sophia asked Murphy if he was going to drop the sails or continue as they were.

"Let's hold our course, kid; I hope we are in friendly waters." The approaching craft was a small fishing boat and it seemed to hold what looked like a collision course with them. It didn't take long for the fishing boat to reach them; at the last minute they gave the sailboat room and passed on their starboard side. After that the fishing boat turned around and cruised in close for what seemed like another look. What now, Murphy thought.

There were three men on deck and they started passing around a pair of binoculars and laughing. Finally Murphy picked up on what was going on; Sophia was still in her bathing suit with a towel over her shoulders. Murphy now knew it was light enough for them to see the girl and Arab men like to dwell on that sort of thing.

"You go below, Sophia, and I'll drive; I think that will get rid of our newfound friends." No sooner than Sophia went below, the fishing boat was turning around and heading out to the Gulf.

Below the water tower that Sophia had been aiming at for so long there appeared to be two jetties; it looked to be about one hundred feet between the two rows of rocks. This was it; he would go for the opening and whatever will be, will be. Calling Sophia back up on deck he gave her the wheel with directions to aim for the center of the opening. Murphy started the engine with no problem; he couldn't help think that something was wrong. He next engaged the transmission and went forward to drop the sails…even that went well. After flaking the main sail on the boom, he tied it off so as not to look sloppy when they pulled into the dock space he hoped to find. Cleaning up the head sail didn't take long and he just got back to the wheel in time to enter the harbor.

The little sailboat began to experience swells that caused it to pitch to port. Murphy corrected: the boat pitched to starboard. Next came the depth sounder alarm, beeping on and off; again the boat pitched to port. This was going to be fun. Murphy grabbed the throttle and pushed it to full power while the depth sounder alarm continued to warn them of impending trouble. At this point they had just entered between the two jetties and had at least seventy five feet to go.

"Hang on down there, little one," Murphy yelled as he corrected the wheel.

Sophia sat down and grabbed the rail. "Are we going to make it, Mr. Murphy?"

"Piece of cake, kid, just hang on."

At one point the sailboat became dangerously close to the port jetty. Bringing her about was all Murphy could do but in the end she did respond. Now the starboard jetty was just on the other side of the rail. Again Murphy pulled the wheel and finally she responded. In the background all they could hear was the depth sounder warning of shallow water; now they were half way through. If they got sideways in the channel and a swell got them, it would be all over. If they hit the bottom during this action, it was worse than over. Again they were pitched to starboard; again Murphy got them back over.

Just as suddenly as it started, it was over. They made it. The depth sounder went quiet and the boat stopped rolling and pitching. They were entering the harbor and Murphy throttled back and took a deep breath.

"Sophia, was that exciting or what?"

Then came the little voice from the cabin, "Are we going to be there soon, I really want to be there soon."

Once again the child caused the two on deck to laugh and they really needed a good laugh.

Murphy spotted a marina off to port and it contained fishing boats of all sizes. Since he was small he figured there must be an open dock for them. Due to the hour there were no fishermen around but he knew that would change shortly; they had to hurry. Pulling into the first empty dock he could find, he remembered he had not set any fenders out, nor dock lines. To slow the sailboat down he put the transmission in reverse and gave it full throttle. It didn't work. When you teach someone to land a boat at a dock Murphy always had one rule of thumb: never approach the dock any faster than you want to hit it. Oh, well. No one saw the little boat hit the dock and fortunately no one was hurt. The passage was over, they made it.

THE REUNION

After securing the boat to the dock Murphy went down below to let the girls know what his next move would be. Rather than walk about the marina with them he suggested that they stay with the boat while he hunted down a phone. It was now 0530 and fishermen were bound to start showing up in full force.

Leaving the two girls in the secured cabin he instructed them to open the companionway for no one but him. As he stepped onto the dock and looked back everything looked normal. There had to be at least seventy five boats in the marina and it was well maintained. At the head of the docks was a building that looked as if it might be the office - no phone booths in sight though. Then it happened; Murphy caught the aroma of coffee, hot coffee. Thinking back on the last twenty hours he seemed to remember Kelly getting him coffee a few times, yet he could not recall drinking any. He could remember drinking soda or water with the girls, but no coffee.

His brain said follow the aroma and you will find coffee and most assuredly, a phone. He walked for a short distance, and behind a large fishing trawler he saw a small trawler with lights on and a man in the cabin. Murphy tapped on the side of the boat and the man looked firsthand and then motioned him aboard.

"Permission to come aboard," Murphy yelled.

"Come aboard, sir."

Murphy boarded and made his way into the cabin.

"Good morning, sir."

The man returned the good morning and asked if he was their charter for today.

"No, sir, I have engine trouble and need to call a mechanic. There is one more thing… could I buy a cup of that coffee?"

The man laughed and reached for another cup, "No, you can't buy a cup of coffee here, it's free."

When the fellow poured the cup of coffee, he handed it to Murphy. The cup felt good in his hands, warm, and the smell.

"Do you take sugar?" the man asked.

Murphy said, yes, and then came the clincher, "One or two sugars?"

Murphy flashed back on yesterday morning with Kelly and it made him smile; here we go again.

"My name is James, sir, James Oman."

"Two sugars, James Oman, and no milk. My name is Smith, Bill Smith."

"What happened to your engine, Mr. Smith?"

"Fuel pump, no big deal. Is there a phone around?"

James pointed toward the bulkhead on the port side and told him he could use that one, "You may not get anyone at this hour though, Mr. Smith."

"I have a friend that I can call and they can take care of it for me. I'll just wait with the boat until they get me help. Do you have a phone book, Mr. Oman?"

"It's your lucky day, Mr. Smith." He reached in the cupboard and that was it.

Murphy put the book on the counter where he was out of the other man's line of sight. Next he took a big sip of coffee. Going to the pages on hotels he found the number for the Coast Hotel. Murphy dialed the number and promptly got the main desk.

"May I have room 363, please."

"One minute, sir."

The phone began to ring, once, twice, three times. All Murphy could think was, please answer, please. Marie Al Fozie had finally fallen asleep. By the seventh ring she answered.

"Hello, is that you, Mr. Murphy?"

This was good, now he didn't have to say his name in front of his new friend.

"Yes it is; we made it." There was a huge pause and then Marie Al Fozie began to cry. It took some time to get her attention but he knew what she must be going through.

"We have engine trouble. Could you send a mechanic to the marina at..." he realized he had no idea of where he was.

"Could you tell me the name of this marina, James?"

"Half Moon Marina, sir"

"We are at Half Moon Marina, do you have that?"

Marie Al Fozie repeated the name, "Why don't you get a cab and come down. I'll wait by the gate for you."

242

"I'll be there as soon as I can, and Mr. Murphy, thank you."

"See you in about thirty minutes."

Murphy thanked James Oman for all his help and went to the main gate, coffee in hand. There was one other thing he had to figure out. Sophia had to be dropped off at the Philippine Embassy. Make that two things, he had to get out of the country also.

REUNION CONTINUED

Michael Murphy stood at the main gate of the marina waiting for Marie Al Fozie and sipping his coffee. So much had taken place in the last day and soon it might be over. Murphy finished his coffee and strolled over to a garbage pail just inside the fence. As he deposited the used paper cup into the pail he noticed all the plastic bags that were stuck on the bottom of the fence. He figured Bahrain had the same problem that Saudi Arabia had; plastic bags decorated any trees, fences, signs, billboards or bushes you may find along the roads. One day someone will come up with a way to prevent the problem but for now, what a mess.

Finally a lone car made its way down the street leading to the marina gate, a taxi. It was a Benz, the preferred vehicle of all taxi companies in the Middle East. Murphy thought how strange it was that people in the United States loved to own a car that served as a taxi here.

The taxi came to a stop and the rear door flew open. He knew that was going to happen. Marie Al Fozie jumped out and ran to him with open arms; he didn't know this was going to happen.

"I thought you would never get here, Michael," as she squeezed him and they almost lost their balance.

"Marie, there were times when I had the same thoughts."

"Where's my baby, where is she?"

On the way to the boat he told Marie to be as calm as she could, he didn't want to attract any attention. The woman said she understood and would indeed be calm. When they reached the little sailboat Murphy stopped her.

The woman wanted to know why they stopped. Murphy pointed to the sailboat.

"She's in the boat?" Murphy nodded yes. At the same time as Murphy nodded yes, the cabin top slid back and the child appeared. Needless to say, once the woman saw her daughter she forgot the part about being calm. As Sophia was attempting to remove the companionway boards, the child was attempting to scramble over Sophia's arms, Marie was attempting to climb into the cockpit and Murphy was attempting to shush everybody.

"Go down below, Marie, please go down below."

The woman did as she was told while Murphy looked around to see if anyone had heard or seen the commotion. So far, so good. Once they were all below decks the hugging and crying aloud went on for some time. Murphy knew they should get out of the marina as quickly as they could, this part was over.

"We have to go, Marie; there will be plenty of time at the hotel to celebrate."

Marie agreed but held the child close, no one was going to separate them this day. She also noticed the young woman that was standing near them.

"I didn't know you had someone to help you, Michael."

"I didn't, Marie, and we don't have time to talk about it now, we have to go."

Murphy locked the boat up after the girls got their clothes on, and they moved onto the dock. He directed Marie to take the girls to the taxi and he would be along momentarily. Looking down at the little sailboat

Murphy felt sad that it should be abandoned after all they had been through. Murphy always said that boats don't have souls but they do have hearts. Time to move on, he thought.

After being dropped off at the hotel, Murphy again told the driver to wait. He would say good-bye to Sophia and send her to the Philippine Embassy. In order not to drag the farewell out, he sent Marie and her daughter up to her room.

Murphy looked the young woman square in the eyes, took her by the shoulders and then pulled her to him, "I couldn't have done this without you, Sophia, and I shall never forget you. I have to send you to the embassy now; you will be safe there. Whatever you do, please don't tell anyone how you got here. We need two days and we will be out of the country. Can you give us two days?"

Sophia looked at the man who just helped her, tears welled up in her eyes and all she could say was, "Thank you, thank you and I shall never forget you, Michael Murphy. Tell Marie I shall miss her, too."

Murphy helped the young girl into the taxi and simply said, "Philippine Embassy." He handed the driver some money and closed the car door. Watching the taxi leave the parking lot was very emotional for Murphy, realizing he didn't even know the young girl's last name.

Joining Marie, Murphy instructed her to call Chris Brown. Tell him what is going on, and tell him to have someone call your husband, from a pay phone, a pay phone that is nowhere near either of your houses. Tell him to inform your husband that your daughter is in New York. When he is ready to see her, he must go through proper channels.

"Do you have a passport for your daughter?"

"Yes and our flight is for tonight at nine o'clock, nonstop to Washington, D.C."

Murphy advised the woman to keep a low profile and say hello to Chris Brown for him. At that point there was nothing left to do but leave. Marie hugged Murphy and thanked him once again.

"You take care of your mom, little one; she loves you."

The child ran to Michael Murphy's side, "Mr. Murphy, where is Sophia?"

"Sophia is on her way home, like you little one. She said to say good-bye and she will miss you."

The child wanted to know when she would see him again, maybe they could play cards.

"I'm never playing cards with you again, little one; you're too good for this old man."

Murphy reached for the door and again realized how hard these goodbyes were getting to be. Without another word being said he left the room; he had to call Kelly.

CPSIA information can be obtained
at www.ICGtesting.com
Printed in the USA
FFOW02n1740040615
13925FF